REUNION

It was six years since Rebel's brother Van
had disappeared—but now at last she had
found him again, in the middle of Aus-
tralia, and was joyfully reunited with him.
But she soon discovered that there was
something very wrong between Van and
Chayne Cavanagh, the man Rebel soon
realised had come to mean more to her
than anyone else. Whose side should she
take?

Books you will enjoy
by KERRY ALLYNE

THE CHALLENGE

Debra was so desperate to get a job—any job—
that she was only too thankful when nice Mrs
McAllister offered her a post as secretary on her
stepson's cattle station in the outback. But she
began to have second thoughts when she actually
met Saxon McAllister. Couldn't she do *anything*
right—or was Saxon just needling her for kicks?

BINDABURRA OUTSTATION

'Go back to the city where you belong,' ordered
Kelly Sinclair contemptuously when Paige made
an impulsive journey from Sydney to the outback. And Paige would by then have been only
too glad to oblige—she didn't want to be in this
disagreeable man's company any longer than she
could help—but fate forestalled her, with disastrous results . . .

SWEET HARVEST

Four years after they had separated, Alix found
herself forced to be once again in the constant
company of her husband Kirby. But any idea of
reconciliation soon vanished as Alix realised that
Kirby had chosen her successor . . .

ACROSS THE GREAT DIVIDE

After being jilted, Nicole would have been glad
of the chance to leave Sydney for Western Aus-
tralia, if it hadn't meant being thrown so much
into the company of the annoying Lang Jamieson.
Yet it was Jerome whom she loved; why was it
Lang who occupied so much of her thoughts?

REUNION AT PITEREEKA

BY
KERRY ALLYNE

MILLS & BOON LIMITED
15–16 BROOK'S MEWS
LONDON W1A 1DR

CHAPTER ONE

'Look, I can guess how miserable things are for you at home with your aunt and uncle, but don't you think you're going a bit too far in even contemplating going off on what will more than likely be a wild goose chase, just because some stranger has answered one of your advertisements and says he met your brother—or who he thinks *might* be the person you're trying to locate—a year ago while he was shearing up in the Flinders Ranges?'

Rebel Hayward looped a long strand of curling, copper-coloured hair behind one ear and eyed her friend with a resolute gaze across the small laminated table which separated them in the coffee lounge.

'But I have to go, Rosemary! It might be my only chance of finding him,' she returned decisively. 'Uncle Roger and Aunt Enid may have brought us up after our parents were killed, but, as you're well aware, it certainly wasn't willingly and it sure hasn't been affectionately! They were happy enough to get their hands on any benefits which might have accrued from taking us in, but we were considered definite liabilities, and they never stopped reminding us of the fact. Six years ago Vandal couldn't stand any more and walked out, and I haven't seen or heard from him since. Now that I have a clue, however slight, as to where he might be, I'm not passing up the opportunity to find him again.'

'But if he hasn't even written to you in all that time, perhaps he—er—would rather not be found,' Rosemary proposed uncomfortably, but feeling it had to be said all the same.

'Oh, no, he would want me to get in touch with him if I could.' The suggestion was vetoed confidently. 'I might not have heard from him, but I don't doubt he's written quite a few times.'

'You mean, you think your aunt and uncle may have kept his letters from you?'

'Not think they may have, know they did,' corrected Rebel promptly, a bitter light entering her dusky-lashed eyes. 'Why else do you think I leased a private box at the post office as an address for any replies to my advertisements? Aunt Enid intercepts and opens all my mail.'

'But why stop his letters from reaching you? What would they gain from that?' her friend queried with a frown.

Rebel laughed cheerlessly. 'Apart from a malicious sense of satisfaction because they were so furious when he left—it deprived them of their chance to get their pound of flesh from him too, you see—but because they also know that there's no way they'll be able to keep me as their cheap labour in Uncle Roger's dingy little antique business if I should happen to discover where Van's living.'

A compassionate nod of understanding followed. Rosemary was fully aware of the hours her companion put in at work, and the pittance she was paid for them. Nonetheless, she regretfully still had to counsel caution.

'But even if that was your brother at—at . . .?' She looked across the table for elucidation.

Rebel scanned the piece of notepaper which had only been in her possession for an hour and which she still held in her hand. 'Deep Wells,' she supplied.

'Well, even if that was him at Deep Wells last December,' Rosemary continued, 'there's no guarantee that he'll still be there now, or that he left a forwarding address if he's moved on.'

'I know,' came the sighed return, followed by a convincing display of shrugged unconcern. 'But it's still the only lead I've got, and I have to start somewhere.'

'You could try one more advertisement. In the Deep Wells newspaper this time,' persuasively.

'Except that I wouldn't have a clue whether the place is

big enough to have its own paper, and by the time I've
made all the appropriate enquiries, inserted the ad and
waited for replies that usually never come, I figure it will be
a whole lot quicker to go there myself and ask around.
More rewarding too, probably.'

'As well as expensive!'

'Yes, well, that's true too, I suppose,' conceded Rebel
with another shrug, and as uncaring as the first. 'But the
little money I've managed to scrape together over the years
is being slowly whittled down by all these advertisements
anyway, and although Uncle Roger refused to allow me to
study for any business qualifications once I left school because he wanted me to work for him, I guess I could find a
job up there if I really had to.'

'In the bush!' Rosemary stared at her, amazed. 'Doing
what?'

'Quite frankly, I don't care much, as long as it's not for
Uncle Roger,' was the quick reply. 'I've only waited until
I was twenty because I've kept hoping I would somehow
hear from Van, or else one of my advertisements would
bear fruit . . . like this.' She waved the letter in her hand
triumphantly.

'Twelve months old fruit, don't forget,' warned the less
venturesome girl opposite her. 'And it's hard enough finding work here in Adelaide. You could find it absolutely
impossible up in the Ranges. Then what would you do,
stranded so far away from anywhere?'

The corners of Rebel's shapely curving mouth turned
down wryly. 'Survive as best I could,' she suddenly grinned
with incorrigible optimism. 'Besides, I'm sick and tired of
putting advertisements in papers and, apart from this one
reply, achieving no result. As far as I can see, the only way
I'm going to locate my brother is if I go out and actually
track him down myself.'

'You make it sound very easy,' mused Rosemary worriedly as she stirred her coffee. 'Whereas, for all you know,
he could very well be in another State by now, or back in
Adelaide even.'

'Uh-uh!' A vehement shake of the head greeted that remark. 'Not the last. If he was back here he would have been in touch somehow.'

'Well, I still think you're mad, quite mad, to propose going to Deep Wells yourself. Goodness, I've never even heard of the place before, let alone know where it is. Do you know?'

This time Rebel's laugh contained quite a deal of amusement as she indicated the letter and teased, 'It's in the Flinders Ranges. Mr Bevan says so.'

'And as they only stretch for some three hundred miles from Port Pirie to Lake Callabonna, it could be anywhere,' the girl across the table retorted with dour exasperation. 'It could even be too small to rate on a map.'

'It doesn't matter much whether it does or not. I'm still going there.'

Realising that nothing she could say was going to dissuade her friend from her plan of action, Rosemary began to turn rueful. 'Up until today I'd always thought you'd been misnamed. Now I'm not so sure. I'm beginning to think that, given the chance, you could be something of a rebel after all.'

'Wouldn't you be too after eleven years of continually being told how much you owed your relatives, and what an unwanted liability you were, etcetera, etcetera?' Rebel questioned drily over the rim of her cup. 'Believe me, even someone as placid and forbearing as yourself would feel like rebelling if you'd had to live in such a repressive atmosphere for as long as I have. God knows how Daddy managed to have a sister like Aunt Enid. I think she must have been a changeling!'

Rosemary smiled, then joked, 'And your brother, is he aptly named too?'

'Vandal?' Even white teeth showed in a wide impish grin. 'According to my aunt he is. She's never forgotten, or forgiven, him for accidentally breaking one of her windows with a tennis ball. You would have thought he'd done it on purpose the way she carried on.'

'Like that time when you slipped over on the back steps and nearly broke your neck and all she was worried about was whether you'd damaged any of her precious eggs you'd been bringing back from the supermarket?'

'Only more so,' with an expressive grimace. A hasty glance at her watch and Rebel gulped down the last of her coffee, folded and put away her invaluable letter, and pushed back her chair. 'I'm sorry, but I'll really have to be going,' she apologised. 'I'm supposed to be picking up a pair of swords—which Uncle Roger will probably con someone into believing are genuine Katana Samurai and accordingly charge the earth for them, the old crook!— but if I'm gone too long he won't stop moaning about it for a week. I'll try and meet you here at the same time on Thursday and let you know how my arrangements are going, okay?'

'Fine by me,' Rosemary smiled, preparing to rise to her own feet. 'When will you tell them you're leaving?'

Rebel exhaled a heavy breath and shook her head slowly. 'I don't honestly know. They may have begrudgingly provided a home, but they did still provide it, so I suppose I owe them something. At the same time, however, I wouldn't put it past them to try and stop me, by any means possible, so I'll have to pick my time carefully whenever I do it.'

'You could just leave a note.'

'Mmm, I could, but I'd rather not if I can avoid it,' she sighed. 'I'll just have to wait and see when my bus or train, or whatever, is due to leave and hope that the right moment presents itself not too many hours beforehand.'

'Well, I wish you luck,' commiserated Rosemary as they paid their bill and headed for the doorway into the street. 'You will write while you're away, though, won't you? You're not planning to cut off communications altogether?'

'No, of course not,' Rebel laughed, and looked fondly at the girl whose friendship over the years had been the one bright spot in her life since her brother's departure. 'I'll keep in touch and let you know exactly what's happening, don't worry.'

'And if you should ever need help, monetary or otherwise, you won't hesitate to let me know that too?'

Affected deeply by the loyal offer, Rebel nodded swiftly.
'Will do,' she murmured huskily, even though she doubted
whether she could ever call on her companion to fulfil such
an offer. It was enough that she had made it.

It didn't take long for Rebel to conclude her arrangements
now that she had made up her mind, and by eight-fifteen
the following Monday morning she had seen her one suitcase of luggage safely stowed in the baggage car and had
taken her seat on the train that she hoped was to carry her
closer to a reunion with her only brother.

Her parting from her aunt and uncle had been just as she
expected—full of verbal abuse, recriminations, denounce-
ments, bitter acrimony, and last but by no means least, a
censorious tirade about not expecting them to take her back
again when she found herself down on her luck and with no
one but strangers to turn to. In the end she had been relieved when her ordered taxi had arrived and she could escape the hostile atmosphere of their house once and for all.

As the day progressed the scenery beyond the window
beside her changed from cities and towns to grassy hills,
then to sugar gum shelter-belted plains. Tree-dotted and
far-reaching open woodlands came next, and as the sun
began its slow slide into the west the view began to alter for
yet another time. They were approaching the rugged north
of the Flinders now, where wattle and mulga covered slopes
gave way to steep mountain ridges and rocky escarpments
which towered over the earth below.

Too keyed up to eat much for dinner—besides, she didn't
want to spend what money she did have on lavish amounts
of food—Rebel returned to her seat from the dining car and
pulled Eric Bevan's letter from her bag in order to read it
again for the third time that day. After nine months of
intermittent advertising for anyone who knew the whereabouts of her brother, his was the only reply she had received. She would have preferred his information to have

been more recent, of course, but at least it was something to go on. At her first reading she had been surprised to learn that Vandal had been shearing in the northern regions of the State, but after thinking it over for a while had come to suppose that maybe it wasn't quite so amazing after all. It was just the sort of thing that would appeal to her devil-may-care, adventure-loving brother.

Beyond the window it was completely dark now, and as she replaced the letter once more in her handbag she knew it couldn't be too long before they reached her destination, and began making sure she had everything collected in readiness. It still seemed to take an interminable time before the train actually started to reduce speed, however, and she was waiting eagerly by the doorway long before they finally pulled into the station.

To her surprise she discovered there were quite a few others leaving the train with her—she had supposed the rest of her fellow passengers would have been going on through Marree and Oodnaddatta to Alice Springs—but as she passed through the ticket barrier into the station yard to await her luggage, she realised from the number of lights twinkling around the area that Deep Wells was somewhat larger than she had anticipated.

Her suitcase delivered, Rebel hired one of the two taxis waiting in the yard to convey her the half mile or so into the centre of town and the hotel she had wired ahead to reserve accommodation on her behalf. It wasn't a particularly large building, she found on arrival, although it was double-storeyed, and as her room opened out on to the encircling balcony the first thing she did on entering it was to throw open the french doors and walk over to the railing.

From there she could get a good view of the main street in either direction and she stood for some time, breathing deeply of the warm night air, and wondering if she could be lucky enough to uncover some additional information concerning Van when she started making her enquiries in the morning. For all she knew he might even be one of those men patronising the bar below, she mused, then shook her head wryly and berated herself for being fanciful. As Rosemary had rightly warned, there was no guarantee he was even in the Deep Wells area still.

Rebel went to bed early that night. Not because she was very tired, but it was the best way she knew to efficiently dispose of those intervening hours until she could begin her investigations and she wanted to be up bright and early in order to make as many enquiries and see as many people as possible. It wouldn't take too many nights at the hotel to severely deplete her finances and she wanted to keep as much of those as she could for travelling expenses.

In the morning, excited as well as enthusiastic, she washed and dressed quickly in a navy blue poplin skirt and white cotton top, and was the first to reach the breakfast room after it had opened. Coffee, toast and marmalade were the only items she selected from the array which had been arranged on the table along one wall, and as the only other person in sight was the young girl who was bringing in the food from the kitchen—she guessed it would probably be an hour or more before the receptionist was on duty at the desk in the lobby—she decided she had nothing to lose by directing her first questions to the waitress. Consequently, when the girl made her next appearance Rebel called across to her.

'Excuse me, but I was wondering if you could help me, please?'

The girl placed the dishes she had been carrying on the table and moved closer, a doubtful expression on her face as she glanced at Rebel's meal.

'Is something wrong?' she asked.

'Oh, no, nothing like that,' Rebel denied with a reassuring smile. 'I thought you might have been able to help me with some local information, that's all.'

'I will if I can,' the other girl smiled, relaxing. 'What did you want to know?'

'Well, I believe there's a sheep station by the name of Tauwangi Downs somewhere hereabouts and I'd like to get in touch with the people who own or run it, only I don't know their name. I thought you might know.'

Twin creases of concentration made an appearance between brown eyes. 'Tauwangi Downs,' the waitress repeated musingly. 'I've heard the name and I think it's a way northwest of here, but I'm sorry, I couldn't tell you who owns it.' An encouraging smile and she suggested helpfully, 'The best people to ask would probably be the stock and station agents down the street. If anyone in town should know, they would.'

'Oh, good, and thank you,' Rebel smiled her appreciation. 'I'll try them as soon as they open.' Her head tilted enquiringly. 'Would you have any idea when that is?'

'Usually about eight-thirty, I think.'

As the girl turned to leave Rebel held up a staying hand. 'One more question before you go. That is ... if you don't mind?' she queried apologetically. And after an acquiescent shake of the head had been given, 'You wouldn't by any chance have heard of a Vandal Hayward working in or around Deep Wells, would you?'

A rueful grin was what she received in response this time. 'I'm sorry, but I can't say I have. Is—is he a relation of yours?' she asked diffidently, and went on to explain, 'I saw your name on the meal card in the kitchen.'

'Yes, he's my brother,' Rebel replied equably. 'Our parents were killed when we were younger and about six years ago we—er—became separated.' There was no point in going into the exact circumstances. 'Then last week I received information saying he'd been working on Tauwangi Downs as a shearer about this time last year, so that's why I'm in town and asking all sorts of peculiar questions,' she concluded with a wry grimace.

'Now I understand,' the young waitress nodded her comprehension. 'And how sad for you. I wish you luck with your search, though.' Once again she made to move away, but on this occasion turned back without being requested. 'I can ask all the hotel staff if they know of him, if you like,' she offered. 'Someone may know something.'

'I'd appreciate it if you could, thank you—er...?'
Winged brows peaked quizzically.

'Ellen—Ellen Olson.'

'And I'm Rebel,' came the immediate return. 'I would be
very grateful, thank you, Ellen. I figure the more people
who know I'm looking for him, the more success I'm likely
to have.'

'Mmm, and with it being such an usual name it's more
likely to stick in people's minds too,' Ellen added.

'Let's hope,' Rebel laughed, and raising her left hand
crossed two fingers. It would be nice to think some good
might eventuate from their both having been christened
with such distinctive names.

Her breakfast finished, Rebel collected her bag from her
room and headed for the street. She still had some time to
kill before the stock and station office would open and she
decided on a leisurely stroll to familiarise herself with the
town while she was waiting. Half an hour was all she needed
to accomplish this—there were, as far as she could make
out, only two streets for shops and businesses—and then
she was forced to cool her heels with as much patience as
she could muster outside the auctioneers' offices until the
staff arrived.

Much to her delight, though, her wait proved to be more
than justified, for when she was finally able to make her
enquiries regarding Tauwangi Downs, and explained her
reason for wanting to contact the property, the younger of
the two men in the office immediately turned to his companion.

'Van Hayward? Isn't that the chap who bought the
Pitereeka store a few months back?' he asked.

And while Rebel held a suspenseful breath, the grey-
haired man on the other side of the counter nodded slowly
and confirmed, 'Yeah, that's the feller. Medium height, a
bit on the thin side, red beard?' He looked at her to see if
the description fitted.

'It sounds as if it could be,' she conceded, although not
without some misgivings.

The only definition of the three which had really depicted her brother was the one concerning his size. Vandal had never been what one would call solidly built. As for the other two.... Well, as she had only been fourteen when he left she had continued to think of him as being much taller than herself, and he certainly hadn't had a beard the last time she saw him. However, though his hair might have been more brown than hers, it did still have a decided red tinge to it and that could account for the colour of the beard he was apparently sporting now.

'And he bought the ...' she hesitated over the word, 'Pitereeka store, you said?'

'That's right,' he endorsed. 'It's about eighty miles or so east of here.'

'How would I get there?' She looked questioningly from one to the other.

'You're travelling on your own?'

She nodded.

'In that case, it would probably be best if you took the Castlefield road and went up from there. It's longer, but it's got a better surface than the one which goes direct from Deep Wells.'

'The only trouble is ... I don't have a car,' she half smiled wryly, and not a little apologetically. 'I came up from Adelaide by train.'

'Oh!' For a moment he looked slightly nonplussed, then he glanced at the younger man. 'Do you know if there's anybody in town from out that way, or who's likely to be going in that direction in the next day or so, Ian?'

A second's meditating thought and the man called Ian shook his head. 'Not except for the mail plane on Thursday,' he supplied in regretful tones.

'Does it take passengers?' Rebel queried swiftly, hope uppermost. It had never occurred to her that transport might prove her greatest barrier to overcome.

'If there's not too much mail and freight, it does.'

That sounded more promising. 'And who do I see about booking a seat?'

'Murray Erskine, the pilot, would be as good as anybody, I guess,' Ian offered with a smile.

'You wouldn't also happen to know where I could find him, would you?' she smiled engagingly back.

'Er—what's today?—Tuesday,' he pondered thoughtfully. 'The hotel dining room at lunch time would probably be your best bet. Or, failing that, you could give him a ring tonight at home. His number's in the book.'

Thanking them both for their assistance, and elated with her unexpected success, Rebel wandered slowly back to the hotel and found them in the middle of hanging their brightly coloured and tinselled Christmas decorations—a sight which brought her to a sudden halt. What with one thing and another she had completely forgotten that Christmas was only a few short weeks away.

Now that she had been reminded, and had also discovered Van's whereabouts, perhaps she ought to see about buying him a present, she decided gaily. Not only would it give her something to do to fill in the remainder of the morning, but she also suspected she would have a far greater choice in Deep Wells than in Pitereeka. As well as that, there wasn't the need for her to conserve her money quite so frugally any more either.

Happy at the mere thought of being reunited with her brother again, Rebel headed back out into the sunlight with a smile on her lips and a lightheartedness in her step. It was all going so much more smoothly than she had imagined! An opinion she was to revise somewhat as she came to discover how hard it was to select a gift for someone she hadn't seen for the last six years. Eventually, she settled on a book as the best way of surmounting the problem because she could recall that he had always liked reading, and anything of a more personal nature she might only be duplicating.

Back at the hotel she took as much time as possible wrapping the present and attaching a card before settling back with the local newspaper—they did have one, after all —and preparing to read it from front to back in an effort to make the time pass more swiftly. Even so, she still had the best part of an hour in which to renew her minimal make-up before she could make her way downstairs for lunch, and she despaired to think that there was still another day and a half of the same to be put in before she could leave for Pitereeka.

Not unnaturally, she was the first to enter the public dining room—as opposed to the breakfast room where she had eaten that morning and which was reserved solely for guests—but she had hardly taken her seat at a small table for two beside one of the windows before Ellen came out to take her order from the unexpectedly varied menu.

'How did it go?' she asked immediately, her dark brown eyes shining with interest. 'Did you get through to Tau-wangi Downs okay?'

'I didn't have to,' Rebel relayed happily with a shake of her head. 'The men in the stock and station agents knew my brother. Apparently he stayed in the district and he's bought the store at a place called Pitereeka.'

'Oh, yes, I know it, although I haven't been out there for some years now,' Ellen smiled, seemingly almost as pleased as Rebel was. 'How marvellous for you to have found him so quickly. I suppose you'll be leaving us this afternoon now, will you?'

'Unfortunately, I can't.' Rebel made a small moue of disappointment. 'I didn't come by car, but I'm hoping to make arrangements to go on the mail plane on Thursday. I was told Murray Erskine, the pilot, would probably be having lunch here today and that I could check with him about it.' Her eyes widened in appeal. 'Could I ask you to point him out to me, please, when he arrives?'

'Of course,' Ellen's assent was readily given. Then, on seeing a frown crease Rebel's smooth forehead, she puzzled, 'Is anything wrong?'

'Not really,' came the half laughing reply in wry tones. 'But it's only just struck me that Vandal's a shopkeeper and, try as I might, I can't quite picture him cheerfully dispensing jars of coffee and packets of washing powder from behind a counter. He always used to be so active, so raring to go, that to even think of him choosing so—so sedate an occupation is beyond my capabilities.'

'Six years is a long time. He could have changed in lots of ways since you last saw him,' Ellen put forward hesitantly.

'And probably has,' sighed Rebel in agreement. 'The same as I have, I suppose.'

As more people entered the dining room and the tables began to fill, Ellen's services were soon required elsewhere, leaving Rebel to wonder by the time she had reached the coffee stage whether Murray Erskine did indeed intend lunching at the hotel that day. She had just about given up hoping for his appearance when Ellen suddenly appeared beside her chair and indicated with a surreptitious nod of her head a man of some thirty years who was still holding the dining room door open while he made a laughing return to someone outside.

'That's Murray,' she whispered. 'The one with the blond hair and the moustache.'

Unaware that he was being so closely observed, the man in question made towards a table set for four, making Ellen hurry into advising, 'It looks as if he's expecting company. He usually sits at that table over there,' motioning to a smaller table further down the room. 'So, if I were you, I'd grab him now while he's still on his own.'

'Thank you, I think I will.' Rebel was on her feet and crossing the room before the pilot could even pick up the menu.

At her approach his brows lifted quizzically above admiring blue eyes and he started to rise.

'No, please, don't get up,' she began, and smiled her thanks when he pulled out a chair so she could sit too. 'And I'm sorry to bother you, but I was told you were the best person for me to see about getting a ride on the mail plane out to Pitereeka on Thursday.'

His lips pursed contemplatively. 'Mmm, I think that could be arranged,' he allowed finally, and then grinned with disarming appeal. 'However, if you don't mind my asking, why would you be wanting to go out there?'

Relief at knowing her transport problems were over put a gay sparkle in her bright blue eyes. 'To see my brother. I'm told he runs the store there.'

'You mean *you're* Van Hayward's sister?'

He not only sounded, but also looked, so amazed that for a moment Rebel could only blink her own surprise. Why it should have caused him such astonishment she had no idea and, in consequence, when she eventually confirmed his supposition it was in a somewhat less than assured voice. But when she would have questioned the reason for the incredulousness in his tone she was prevented by the arrival of another two men.

The elder of the two caught and held her attention first and she did a rapid summary. Early thirties, tall, broad of shoulder and lean of hip. Almost jet black hair above a wide and intelligent forehead, and a pair of watchful hazel-green eyes which seemed to miss nothing. A finely moulded yet surprisingly strong nose, and a wryly turned mouth which hinted at an innate self-confidence. The cleft chin didn't merely hint, though, it shouted of strength and authority. All in all, she concluded ruefully, in mind and body he was as alert and supple as one of the large cat family ... and just about as dangerous!

The younger man exuded nowhere near the same intense masculinity, she noted with relief, although there was a certain similarity about their features, and he was certainly almost as tall and as muscular as his companion. She guessed him to be only a few years older than herself, his hair more brown than black, his eyes a definite brown. It was around the lower half of his face that the resemblance between the two of them was most noticeable, only in this instance the countenance was rather more youthful than forceful. With a start she realised the pilot was making introductions.

'Miss Hayward, allow me to introduce Chayne,' he gestured to the taller man first, 'and Scott Cavanagh. Miss

Hayward is ...' and Rebel could have sworn there was a deliberate pause before he completed, 'Van Hayward's sister.'

'Good lord!'

The stunned outburst from Scott Cavanagh brought a wry twist to the blond man's lips, but Chayne Cavanagh's steady regard never wavered from Rebel's face as she self-consciously broke off her softly spoken acknowledgement to stare at the younger man confusedly. Just what was going on here? That was the second time in almost as many minutes that someone had shown surprise at her relationship to Van.

'I'm sorry, I just wasn't expecting that,' Scott immediately apologised, trying to make amends for the obvious bewilderment he had put into the eyes gazing up at him so disconcertingly. 'Van has—I mean, we—er ...'

'What my brother is unsuccessfully trying to say,' inserted Chayne Cavanagh in a deep-timbred voice, 'is that Van has spoken about you so often—but, unfortunately, without a scrap of evidence to prove your existence—that people have, I'm afraid, tended to think he was having them on.'

'Well, I can assure you I'm no mirage!' Her retort was indignantly made, and as much on her brother's behalf as her own.

Against the darkly bronzed colour of his skin his teeth gleamed shining white. 'Of that, at least three of us are now very well aware,' he drawled lazily as his eyes swept over her curving figure in a thorough appraisal.

A stain of bright pink suffused Rebel's cheeks and she lowered her gaze, flustered. During the time she had spent in her aunt and uncle's house she hadn't been allowed to lead a particularly social life, and someone of this man's undoubted experience with the opposite sex was completely beyond her knowledge. She just didn't have the necessary sophistication to counter his kind of provoking wordplay and she knew it! She turned to the man beside him, anxious to escape from his friend's disturbing presence as soon as possible.

'A-about that flight, Mr Erskine,' she reverted to the reason for her being there. 'Who do I pay, and how much?'

'You'd better leave it till Thursday and fix me up at the office at the airstrip,' he shrugged casually. 'It's so long since I've carried a passenger out that way that I've forgotten what the charge is.'

'Isn't Van coming in to pick you up, then?' Scott inserted, brows lifting.

She shook her head a little shyly. 'No, he isn't even aware that I'm here in Deep Wells. I want to surprise him.' Swinging the pilot's way once more she surprised an unspoken message passing between him and Chayne Cavanagh and, thinking they were probably anxious for her to leave so they could resume their own conversation, she hurriedly gained her feet. 'I—I'm sorry to have taken so much of your time,' she apologised stiltedly. 'What time shall I meet you at the airport on Thursday?'

'Why not join us and we can discuss it over lunch?' Murray suggested.

'Oh, no ... thank you,' she rejected the offer promptly. Then, fearing she might have sounded ungracious, added, 'It's very kind of you, but really, there's no need. Besides ...' waving a hand towards her own table, 'I've just about finished.'

'We can't persuade you?'

Rebel hadn't noticed either of the other two even trying. Not that she wanted them too, of course!

'No, thank you,' she smiled faintly, shaking her head. 'But if you could just tell me what time I should be at the airport...?'

'Oh, a little before seven, I guess. I normally take off around then.' His blue eyes twinkled attractively. 'You're sure you won't join us?' He tried one final time to change her mind.

She laughed—a melodious, bubbling sound—but still

refused, and began walking away. No sooner had she returned to her table than Ellen appeared like a magic genie. She had obviously been hovering anxiously in the background while Rebel made her arrangements.

'Is it all set?' she enquired eagerly.

'Mmm, I leave on Thursday at seven o'clock.'

Ellen's eyes covertly surveyed the other side of the room. 'I saw you with the Cavanaghs,' she grinned. 'What did you think of them?'

Involuntarily, Rebel's eyes swung in the same direction, connected with a perturbing hazel-green gaze which sent trickles of inexplicable unease along her spine, as well as flags of scarlet into her cheeks, and glanced swiftly away.

'I—er—they seemed pleasant enough,' she told the girl next to her with a forced indifference. 'Who are they, anyway? Do they live in Deep Wells?'

'Oh, no!' Ellen gave a vigorous denying shake of her head. 'They come from Mount Cavanagh Station, just outside Pitereeka. I expect you'll be seeing quite a lot of them while you're staying with your brother, what with it being Christmas and all.' She exhaled a heavily heartfelt breath. 'Lucky you!'

Uncertain that she wanted to see more of them—at least the older one!—Rebel frowned. 'Why should Christmas make a difference?'

'Because of all the parties, naturally! Everyone has them and everyone, but everyone, goes to them.' Ellen tipped her head sideways to peer at Rebel in amazement. 'Don't you have them too in Adelaide?'

'Oh, yes! Yes, of course,' she smiled back quickly, remembering how it had been when her parents were still alive and before her aunt and uncle could forbid her to attend any such degenerate frivolities, as they called them.

Someone signalled for Ellen's attention and with a reluctant grimace she was off about her duties again, while Rebel's eyes slid waywardly back to a particular table near the door. Happily, there was no return gaze this time and for a few moments she watched the three men's changing expressions as they continued with their meal and their conversation. Their reactions on learning of her connection with Van still troubled her for some unknown reason, and although Chayne Cavanagh's explanation should have satisfied her, somehow it hadn't. Perhaps because it had been just a little too pat, she decided with hindsight, or perhaps ...

She came out of the reverie she had unwittingly fallen into with an embarrassed flickering of her eyes. Oh, God, she'd done it again! This was the second time now she had been discovered staring across at their table, and if she wasn't careful she would have them imagining she had regretted her decision not to join them and was hoping for another invitation. In a flurry of movement she gathered up her bag and prepared to leave. The best way to dismiss any such thoughts from their minds was to remove herself from their vicinity altogether!

The briefest of stiff smiles was all she directed towards them as she passed their table on her way to the door, but even though she could find no fault with their courteous acknowledgments, by the time she reached the hotel lobby her face felt traitorously warm and her breathing was anything but calm.

On impulse she went straight to the cigarette vending machine, inserted the required number of coins, and picked up the automatically released packet with impatient fingers. Normally she didn't smoke—she had always preferred to spend what little money she did have on more necessary items—but this afternoon she felt in dire need of something to settle her strangely quivering nerves, and to help dispel the image of an arresting male face from her mind.

CHAPTER TWO

REBEL spent most of the afternoon in her room writing to Rosemary—a long screed telling her almost word for word what had happened since she had left Adelaide the day before—doing some washing, and reading the paperback she had bought for herself that morning. She would have liked to have driven out of town to see some more of the surrounding district, but as she didn't possess a car and there were no tourist buses, it seemed she was going to have to be content to confine herself to the hotel and Deep Wells' two shopping streets for the rest of her stay.

In contrast to the lunch crowd, the dining room was practically deserted when she went down for her final meal of the day. There wasn't even Ellen to pass a few words with either, because that girl was busily helping to set everything up in readiness for one of the parties she had mentioned, and which was apparently to be held in the hotel's beer garden that evening.

Afterwards, she went for a walk around the block, twice, and then disconsolately returned to her room where she tried to regain some interest in her book. As darkness began to fall, however, and the sound of laughter, clinking glasses, and merriment began floating up from the party below, it became increasingly difficult for her to concentrate and, lighting another cigarette, she wandered out on to the balcony to stare unseeingly into the street beneath. She was becoming tempted to telephone Van just for the opportunity of talking to someone!

The first time she heard the knocking noise coming from behind her she ignored it, but when it came again a few seconds later, and louder, she whirled around and hurried back into her room. It was her door someone was knocking at! Opening it, she took a surprised step backwards at finding Scott Cavanagh facing her.

24

'I've come to take you to a party,' he announced without any preliminaries, but with a wide and winning smile. 'And I've been told I'm not allowed to take no for an answer.'

'Oh?' Rebel looked at him questioningly, part amused, part wary. 'Who by?'

'Does it matter?'

She supposed it didn't, but as much as she felt she would like to join the celebration, it was almost two years since she had last been to a party, something held her back and she suddenly found herself shaking her head and murmuring regretfully, 'It was very kind of you to think of me, but really I . . .'

'Uh-uh!' He wagged a finger at her remonstratively. 'No excuses will be accepted. Besides, you couldn't sleep with all the noise going on, anyway.'

It was no more than the truth, but still she was doubtful. His brother had left her feeling so out of her depth at lunch time that she was extremely chary of having the experience repeated.

'Come on, Rebel! It is Rebel, isn't it?' he sought confirmation with a grin when she still hadn't said anything. A verifying nod and he continued, 'It's just a party to celebrate Christmas. There's no sinister motive behind the invitation, I can assure you.'

Nothing could have been further from her mind and she burst into a hasty denial. 'Oh, it didn't occur to me to suppose there was!'

'Well, then?' He spread his hands expressively, and invitingly, wide.

'All right! I will come, thank you,' she capitulated suddenly with an answering smile. Why shouldn't she go? She was free to make her own decisions now. There was no Aunt Enid or Uncle Roger to forbid her attendance any more, and so what if Chayne Cavanagh was there? She could always ignore him, couldn't she?

'Shall we join the others?' Scott held out his arm towards her.

Rebel glanced down at the slim-fitting halter-necked

dress of sea green and oatmeal rayon she had changed into
for dinner. 'Is this okay to wear?' she queried uncertainly.
Although Scott was casually outfitted in slacks and open-
neck shirt, that didn't necessarily mean that the women
wouldn't be gowned a little more formally.

'Sure!' he endorsed promptly, his brown eyes making an
appreciative assessment. 'You look fine to me.'

'In that case . . .' Turning, she pushed a few things into a
white envelope purse, then took his proffered arm. 'Let's
go,' she suggested gaily.

In the beer garden there were people everywhere and
Rebel suspected that the whole of Deep Wells and its
environs had turned out in force for the occasion. Tables
and chairs were clustered together in groups amid tall trees
and flowering shrubs, while brightly coloured streamers,
balloons, and lanterns gave it a decidedly festive air. A
section of the concreted floor had been left empty for dancing, and away in one corner the youthful members of the
band were beginning to tune their instruments energeti-
cally, bringing a smile to Rebel's lips. As her companion
had forecast, once they got started it would have been impossible to sleep, anyway!

Acknowledging greetings as he went, Scott led her between tables and around shrubs until they reached one a
little further away from the thickest press of the crowd,
and she swiftly took note of the occupants. There was
Murray Erskine—Scott's brother, of course!—and a tall,
haughty-featured blonde whose dream of a gown of
mushroom-coloured chiffon had Rebel immediately questioning her wisdom in being persuaded to join the party.
These people were obviously in a class of their own, and
an evening spent in their company could prove not only
discomfiting, but extremely mortifying as well.

As they drew near to the table the two men rose to their
feet and, pulling out a chair for her, Scott smiled amiably.
'You know Murray and Chayne, of course, but this very
chic young lady,' indicating the blonde, who was scrutinis-

ing Rebel with distinctly cool blue eyes, 'is Karina Loudon, a friend of the family. Karina, I'd like you to meet Rebel Hayward. She's come up from Adelaide to see her brother,' he added for the other girl's benefit.

'Oh?' Karina stared curiously across the table as the men re-seated themselves. 'I can't recall any family by the name of Hayward owning a property around Deep Wells.'

Seeing the older girl hadn't felt obliged to offer a greeting, Rebel decided to forgo that courtesy as well. 'Probably because he doesn't own a property around Deep Wells. Just the store at Pitereeka,' she revealed in a dry tone.

'Then that explains why I've never heard of him, of course! The only use I have for Pitereeka is to drive straight through it on my way to Mount Cavanagh,' Karina laughed, disparagingly in Rebel's estimation, before turning to smile sympathetically at the man beside her. 'That's where you come in, my love, is it? You having been prevailed upon to provide the transport, I suppose.'

Rebel drew in a sharply resentful breath, but before she was able to refute the allegation Murray had already begun a grinned disclaimer. 'Ah, but that's where you're wrong, Karina. *I'm* the fortunate one providing the transport, not Chayne.'

Karina looked as if she couldn't care less who was providing it, as long as it wasn't the dark-haired man whose arm she was clutching so possessively.

'Though, of course, we would have offered to do the honours if we hadn't been heading south for a couple of days,' Scott half turned in his seat to assure Rebel earnestly.

A statement she accepted with a strained smile before declaring firmly, 'But which I wouldn't have accepted.' Her head lifted proudly and her eyes flashed with a blue fire as she stared directly at the man opposite—for the first time that evening. 'I didn't come up here expecting people to do me any favours. I came intending to pay my own way, and that's what I mean to continue doing.'

His girl-friend sniffed disinterestedly, but Chayne's

ebony-lashed eyes returned her challenging gaze with un-wavering tenacity. 'And if that should suddenly become impossible?' he enquired softly.

For a moment her glance faltered slightly. 'I don't know what you mean,' she puzzled.

'I mean that circumstances have a habit of changing, honey,' he explained with a sardonic intonation which brought a betraying warmth to her cheeks. 'And sometimes it's wiser to accept help than to issue a blanket refusal.'

If he was implying that it wasn't politic to knock back an offer of assistance from the influential Cavanaghs then he was in for a surprise, because it didn't matter to her one iota! Just who did they think they were, anyhow? She leant back in her chair and her annoyance gave her the confidence to eye him rebelliously.

'I'll try and keep it in mind,' she mocked. 'But in the meantime, if I *should* need assistance, then I'm sure my brother will be only too willing to provide it rather than have me rely on strangers.'

'Not strangers, honey,' he corrected immediately. 'Neigh-bours!'

And probably customers of Van's too! Rebel swallowed hard and hoped she hadn't said anything that might have a detrimental effect on her brother's business. It was all very satisfying to attempt to put Chayne Cavanagh in his place, but at the same time she wouldn't like to alienate those who, for all she was aware, could be Van's most valued clients. Consequently, when Scott broke in on her musings a few seconds later to ask her to dance now that the band had started playing, she accepted with alacrity.

'You know, Rebel, that was good advice Chayne gave you,' he counselled as soon as they found a small space in which to move to the music. 'It's a way of life to help your neighbour out here, and one of these days you might find that you would—er—appreciate some assistance.'

'In other words, whatever he offers I have no choice but to accept, whether I want to or not, is that it?' she charged disdainfully.

'Not exactly.' He moved his head decisively. 'Although it might be as well for you to remember that the system cuts both ways.'

'Meaning?'

'Only that we are also obliged to offer our help, whether we want to or not!'

'I see,' she nodded thoughtfully, her disco steps taking her away from him and then back again so she could voice her next query. 'Is that also the reason I was invited to this party? Because of a sense of obligation?'

'But only of a personal nature,' he suddenly grinned, causing Rebel to eye him quizzically. Whereupon he enlightened her, 'We'd be fools to ourselves if we didn't invite one of the best looking females in town, now, wouldn't we?'

It was a compliment and yet, contrarily, she couldn't leave it at that. 'What if I'd been plain?' she just had to probe.

A wry speculation eased its way over Scott's face as his head angled to one side. 'Are you looking for a fight, lady?' he half laughed, half frowned.

'Wh-what makes you say that?'

'Your attitude mainly,' he returned drily.

Creamy cheeks reddened and Rebel came to a complete halt, her expression troubled, her head downbent. Knowing he was right didn't make it any easier. 'I'm sorry,' she apologised in a low voice, and flicking him a contrite glance. 'I'm not usually so disagreeable and difficult to get along with.'

'So what makes tonight different?' he teased gently, curiously.

A shrug and her eyes came up to meet his ruefully this time. 'That's just the problem ... I don't really know.' At least not as far as Scott was concerned. His brother was something quite different, however.

'Then how about we try starting again, hmm?'

'You don't have to, if you'd rather not,' she murmured in a deprecatory manner. 'I—I'll understand.'

'Don't be an idiot!' he chided, and tipped her face up to his. 'I know just the thing to send that woebegone look on its way too.' He smiled and, catching hold of her hand in his, began leading her between the rest of the dancers.

At the bar he ordered a beer and a champagne cocktail, the latter which he presented to Rebel along with the bantering observation, 'There! That should help give your spirits a lift.'

'Not too high, I hope,' she grimaced wryly, and took an experimental sip. It was the first time she had ever tasted champagne and she wasn't quite sure what to expect.

'Okay?' Scott eyed her glass enquiringly.

'Lovely,' she approved wholeheartedly as she settled herself on a stool and prepared to enjoy the rest of it.

Scott remained standing, one well polished shoe resting on the foot-rail, one brown forearm resting on the top of the bar. 'How come you've never been to see your brother before this, Rebel?' he asked unexpectedly.

When she had recovered from her surprise she replied simply and honestly. 'Because until last week I had no idea where he was.'

'But he says he's written to you ... many times.'

That surely wasn't an accusing note she could detect in his voice? No, it couldn't possibly be; she rejected the idea almost as soon as it occurred. But his words did serve to confirm what had only been supposition when she had mentioned the matter to Rosemary. Her aunt and uncle had kept his letters from her!

'Well, if he did, I'm afraid I didn't receive them,' she shrugged. After Thursday it wouldn't matter any more whether they had reached her or not.

'Yet you knew where to reach him when *you* wanted to.'

This time the emphasis was too strong for her to dismiss it so swiftly and she returned his gaze questioningly, if a little bewilderedly. 'Just what are you accusing me of, Scott?'

'I wasn't aware I was accusing you of anything,' he began, then halted abruptly and sighed. 'No, that's not completely true, is it? I guess I was accusing you, and I'm sorry. It's none of my business and I've got no right.'

That might have been true, but Rebel needed clarification now even more than she had before. 'But—but what is it that I'm s-supposed to have done?' she stammered in her confusion. The last of her champagne cocktail disappeared in one fortifying mouthful.

'Nothing,' he denied with a covering grin as he signalled to the barman. 'So you can stop looking so worried.'

'No, please!' She caught at his arm and swung him back to face her. 'Scott, I want to know!' she tried to compel him into answering.

'There's nothing to know.' He adamantly refused to be drawn any further on the subject.

Rebel stared at him impotently and, without conscious thought, picked up the new glass the barman placed in front of her and began drinking from it as she thought back over what had been said.

'Oh, no, he couldn't!' she exclaimed incredulously a few seconds later. 'Van surely doesn't think I deliberately didn't bother to answer his letters, does he?' Her eyes sought those of the man in front of her as she repeated a disbelieving, 'Does he, Scott?'

Broad shoulders were hunched in an offhand gesture. 'He mentioned something of the kind once,' he divulged finally, but immediately went on to justify, 'Although he'd had a few drinks at the time, so it's quite possible he didn't mean what he said.'

'No?' She sent him a speaking glance. 'You obviously believed him.'

'Only after a fashion. I don't think anyone believed him fully. You seem to forget that none of us were even sure you existed,' he reminded her in wry accents.

Taking another sip of her drink, Rebel viewed him steadily over the rim of her glass. 'Then why were you so quick to accuse me a few moments ago?'

'Because I was probably doing exactly the same as Van did, and letting the beer do my talking for me,' he grinned.

'You've only had one!'

'Since dinner.'

'Since dinner?' she echoed, not quite certain of his meaning.

'That's right,' he endorsed with a broadening smile. 'Before dinner ... well, that was another matter.'

'Oh, I see.' She tried to look disapproving but couldn't quite make it and ended by laughing instead. With a glass of wine in her own hand and a delightful sense of well-being overtaking her with each passing minute, she was hardly in a position to pass judgment.

'I thought you two were dancing. Or have you decided on a private party of your own?' A voice Rebel couldn't mistake sounded lazily behind her.

'No, we're just reinvigorating ourselves for our next effort,' Scott returned humorously.

Rebel swivelled around on her stool, thankfully noting that Karina was nowhere in sight—she really didn't think that girl was going to make her list of favourite people—and, bolstered by that pervading feeling of lightheartedness, was able to gaze upwards at Chayne Cavanagh's bronzed features without succumbing to the nervous awareness which had disconcerted her so annoyingly on all previous occasions.

'And doing it very successfully too, I might say,' she added vivaciously, her blue eyes sparkling brightly within their dark frame of long curling lashes. 'I feel distinctly cheered and refreshed.'

'You don't say!' Chayne's firm-lipped mouth began to curve in amusement, although his forehead was creasing suspiciously as he looked to his brother. 'Just what have you been giving her to cause this so refreshed state?' he quizzed.

Scott started to laugh and held up one hand in a disclaiming movement. 'Scout's honour, two champagne cocktails, that's all,' he vowed.

The gist of their conversation was all too apparent and, drawing herself up to her full height, Rebel fixed the elder of the two with as haughty a glare as she could manage.

'I may be a little relaxed, Mr Cavanagh, but I am certainly not intoxicated, if that's what you're trying to imply!' She finished her drink and replaced the glass on the counter prior to jumping to her feet. 'See! I can walk as straight a line as you can!' she declared defiantly, and set off for the other end of the bar in order to prove her point.

She hadn't travelled more than a few yards before her wrist was encircled lightly, but securely, by lean powerful fingers as Chayne drew abreast of her, smiling lazily.

'Okay, you've convinced me. You may not be intoxicated at the moment, honey, but if you're that unused to wine, then you sure as hell will be if you don't leave a longer space between your next two drinks.'

Not that she considered it any of his business how much or how often she had a drink, Rebel still couldn't resist casting him a deeply taunting glance. 'Advice born of personal experience ... or a command, Mr Cavanagh?' she challenged.

'Chayne,' came the prompt correction.

Earlier she might have quibbled over the use of his first name, but not now. 'All right, then ... Chayne,' she acceded with surprising docility.

'As to your question ...' He shrugged indolently. Although his eyes weren't quiescent, she noted. They threatened all manner of reprisals and she experienced an inward shiver—heaven help her, it surely wasn't of excitement!— as she momentarily contemplated the form they might take. 'Would I dare try to command someone who, apparently, isn't even given to accepting offers of help?'

'It certainly looks like it,' she half grimaced sardonically on finding herself being turned into his arms so they could move slowly in time to the softly haunting tune the band was now playing. 'I don't remember being given the choice as to whether I wanted to dance or not. Or don't you believe in allowing anyone the opportunity to refuse you?' she dared to provoke.

His ensuing smile was so fascinatingly shaped that it took

some time for her to realise they had come to a halt and
that he had taken a step away from her, his hands outspread
to indicate she was at liberty to leave. She was too occupied
in struggling to counter the devastating effect he was having
on her nervous system.

'Feel free,' he invited in a lazy drawl.

Rebel stared up at him uncertainly, her bottom lip caught
between her teeth, and all her old feelings of inadequacy
when confronted by this man returning in full force. Now
what did she do? She hadn't really been objecting to his
action, merely wanting to prove—to herself as much as
anyone—that she could trade taunts with him and remain
completely unmoved by his disturbing presence while she
did so. Only she hadn't succeeded on either count, she reflected ruefully, and meanwhile he was waiting for an answer. Dropping her gaze to the vicinity of his broad chest,
she hunched one shoulder uncomfortably.

'I'm sorry,' she murmured, and turning to leave remembered Scott's remark, which she offered excusingly. 'I think
I've been letting those two glasses of champagne do too
much of my talking for me.'

Two warm hands unexpectedly cupped her face and prevented her from moving further away. 'You didn't have to
tell *me* that, honey,' Chayne laughed down into her slightly
bemused eyes. When she didn't reply—she was finding it
difficult enough just to hold his amused gaze—he shook
his head in a mixture of exasperation and disbelief. 'Oh,
God! You really are an innocent, aren't you? What on
earth were your parents thinking of when they let you come
up here on your own?'

Dismayed to think her inexperience was so obvious,
Rebel pulled out of his grasp and tried to disguise it with a
façade of cool indifference. 'No one *let* me come here, I'm
old enough to make my own decisions. In any case, my
parents are dead,' she concluded stiffly.

'Recently?'

'No, eleven years ago, as a matter of fact.'

Chayne accepted her information with a thoughtful nod,

then motioned with his head towards the dance floor. 'Would you care to dance, Miss Hayward?' he enquired, lightly teasing.

'Thank you.' Her assent was selfconsciously but determinedly made. She couldn't keep running away from him every time he made her feel unsettled and unsure of herself or she would never be anything but the immature adolescent he clearly considered her to be.

For a time they circled the floor in silence and Rebel used the opportunity thus provided to concentrate on her movements. She was out of practice with this style of dancing and she didn't want to make a complete fool of herself by missing her step and stumbling gauchely. Of course, being as conscious as she was of her partner's hand resting against the bare skin of her back wasn't aiding her contemplation any. In fact, it was downright distracting!

'How long is it since you've seen your brother, then, Rebel?' Chayne's query abruptly claimed her attention.

'Six years.' And because of Scott's near-accusation earlier, her head lifted to an almost defiant pose with her countering, 'Why?'

Wide shoulders moved negligently beneath their covering of old-gold silk knit and the corners of his mouth crooked attractively. 'Nothing in particular, except that I hope you're prepared for any changes which might have occurred in that time.'

'Oh, yes,' she smiled happily, relieved. 'Especially after what I was told about him this morning.'

'Which was?'

There was a thread of—wariness?—in his tone which immediately made her doubly so and had her searching his unrevealing expression nervously. 'That he apparently now wears a beard,' she relayed tentatively.

Chayne nodded and smiled easily, although Rebel was positive she wasn't mistaken in thinking there had been a significant breath expelled along with it. 'That's right, he started to grow it earlier in the year when he decided on a change from shearer to stockman.'

And now a storekeeper! 'He obviously didn't stay as a stockman for long, then,' she speculated.

'No, I don't think the work was quite what he was anticipating.'

'And yet I can't really envisage him being happy in a shop either,' she continued in the same musing manner. 'That is, unless he's changed far more than I realise.' Looking up quickly, she half smiled and urged, 'Please tell me just what he is like. You seem to know him quite well.'

'Not really.' His denial was so unequivocal that she frowned. 'Most of my knowledge of Van is hearsay, not first-hand.'

'Oh, but you must ... I mean, surely you talk to him when you go in the store,' she persevered.

'Sorry, honey, but I haven't been in the Pitereeka store for months.'

Rebel's blue eyes widened in amazement. 'But don't you buy your supplies there?'

The wry twist of his lips set her heart pounding heavily against her ribs. 'Apart from the fact that it doesn't happen to be one of my duties to purchase the household supplies —our housekeeper does that—we prefer to buy them in Deep Wells,' he advised in a somewhat mocking drawl.

'Well, I hardly think that's very loyal of you,' she reproached breathlessly. When he looked at her in that provoking fashion how could she possibly remain unaffected? 'I would have imagined it was to your advantage to purchase them from somewhere closer to hand.'

'Would you now?' His eyes seemed to be nearly pure green as a laughing light appeared in their depths. 'Then maybe we'll have to see if we can't get Doris to change her shopping habits while you're in town, hmm?'

Doris being their housekeeper, she surmised, and sent him a glance which was equally, if unknowingly, taunting. 'I'll hold you to that,' she promised. Seeing they obviously weren't Van's customers already, as she had mistakenly believed previously, then it was the least she could do for her brother to try and ensure they became so. 'When may we expect your first order?'

White teeth showed in a wide, tantalising smile. 'When you're there to deliver it personally.'

Rebel couldn't quite decide whether he was making fun of her or not, but for Van's sake she pressed on regardless, retorting in the same bantering tone, 'I'm sure that can be arranged any time after Thursday, provided ...' From the corner of her eye she saw Karina Loudon whirl past in the arms of another man and gulped hastily on recognising the venomous look in the other girl's eyes. Karina plainly wasn't happy at being denied the company of her escort for so long! Another swallow and she continued as airily as she could. 'Now where was I? Oh, yes ... provided, of course, that you're there to accept it, personally.'

'Why me, in particular?'

'So you can see and judge the standard of our service for yourself, naturally!'

'And if I'm dissatisfied?'

'Then we'll do everything within our power to make certain you are satisfied.' Van would doubtless go along with that in order to gain their business, which she guessed would be quite considerable. 'There must be all sorts of inducements we can offer that they can't in Deep Wells.'

'Such as?' drily.

'Oh—er ...' It had only been a spur of the moment idea and as she cast about for a suitable reply she looked flustered for a few seconds. Then she crossed her fingers and hoped she was correct in thinking Ellen had said their property wasn't far from town. 'Same day service!' she blurted triumphantly. 'I bet you don't often get that from Deep Wells ... if ever!'

'And as we usually buy our supplies in bulk, it's very rare that we need it,' he lazily, but effectively, squashed her elation.

Now that was something she hadn't considered. But not to be balked entirely, she pressured, 'You do sometimes, though?'

'It has been known to happen.'

Rebel pulled back slightly in his arms, her head tilting to one side, her expression wry in the extreme. 'You sure don't intend for me to become flushed with success, do you?'

'Not at my expense, I don't,' he laughed. 'This is business, honey, not an exercise in philanthropy.'

So he had only been making fun of her after all. 'You never even meant to give us a try, did you?' she charged disappointedly, and a little resentfully.

His arms held her closer in order to swing them out of the path of another couple, and then he shrugged. 'I wouldn't say that. If you can provide comparable prices and delivery—and I mean *you*, personally—then I'll consider it.'

Under the circumstances she supposed it was the best she could have hoped for, although his wording did cause a faintly perplexed furrow to etch its way across her forehead. 'Why me? Why not Van?' she puzzled curiously. 'It is his store, after all, and I wouldn't like him to think I was trying to take over.'

Chayne didn't look the slightest bit interested in what Van thought. 'Take it or leave it, honey, but that's the deal,' he announced indifferently.

'But you still haven't told me why,' she frowned, confused more than ever by the finality in his tone.

'Maybe because you're prettier than he is.'

'Oh, don't try fobbing me off with some patronising remark like that!' she rounded on him sarcastically, her annoyance at his evasion coming to the fore. 'I asked a serious question and I'd like a serious reply.'

'Then put it down to a personal idiosyncrasy of mine,' he recommended tautly. 'If I discuss a deal with someone, I prefer to follow the matter through with that particular person, and only that person. I've found it generally causes less complications that way.'

Perfectly believable, Rebel was willing to allow, and yet . . . 'Including delivery?' she quizzed askance.

'In this instance, yes.' That nerve-tingling look of devilment was back in his eyes. 'You *are* prettier than your brother.'

'I sh-should hope so.' Her half stammered attempt at mock indignation did absolutely nothing to cover her self-consciousness, and therefore it was with a thankful sigh of relief that she realised the dance had come to an end and she could return to the table without giving him any further opportunity to disconcert her.

The rest of the evening passed swiftly and pleasantly for Rebel as she either danced with Scott or Murray, and on a couple of occasions with friends of theirs who had obviously approached their group with the sole intention of making her acquaintance. Chayne, however, made no move to invite her on to the floor a second time—she suspected Karina Loudon had seen to that!—and although she wasn't at all sure whether she was breathing easier, or heavier, due to the omission, she refused to let it spoil her enjoyment.

It was the very first party she had ever attended where she hadn't had a curfew placed on her, or been soundly berated for wanting to go in the first place, and she meant to savour every last minute of it. She accepted more champagne cocktails from Scott, albeit defiantly under his elder brother's eye, but judiciously spacing them further apart this time. She even tried to be friendly to Karina, but when this showed little sign of success, accepted the other girl's rebuffs with equanimity. Nothing was going to ruin this evening for her, and especially not Chayne's supercilious girl-friend!

Eventually, though, it had to come to an end, and it was with a small sigh of regret that she heard the band play their last number and saw the various groups in the beer garden beginning to take their leave. At some time during the evening Murray apparently had discovered someone he was anxious to escort home, and after he had made his excuses and bade them goodnight, Rebel turned to Scott with a smile.

'I can see myself back to my room,' she said. 'There's no need for you to bother.'

'He'd better!'

The words snapped forth from Chayne with such intensity that Rebel looked at him in wide-eyed surprise, as did Karina, although Scott merely grinned and held up a placatory hand.

'Don't panic,' he exhorted. 'I fully intended to see Rebel to her room.'

A few moments later, as they mounted the stairs together, Rebel again turned to the man accompanying her. 'Does Chayne often tell you what to do like that?' she frowned.

Seemingly the least concerned over the incident, Scott laughed. 'Not usually, although it wasn't entirely unexpected with the problems he's got on his plate at the moment.'

'Oh?' Chayne Cavanagh hadn't struck her as a man with worries, but now her inquisitiveness was piqued and she couldn't refrain from seeking to have it satisfied. 'What sort of problems?'

'All sorts.'

A not particularly enlightening answer, nor a satisfactory one as far as Rebel was concerned, and trying her best not to look too interested she was forced into saying, 'With regard to your property, I suppose?'

'What makes you say that?'

Without warning she suddenly found herself looking into a pair of remarkably suspicious brown eyes and hastily she tried to reassure him. 'I—er—no particular reason. I just took a guess, that's all.' Her own gaze was apologetic. 'I'm sorry, Scott, I shouldn't have pried.'

'No, you're okay,' he waved aside her apology wryly. 'I should have realised you couldn't know anything about what's going on. It's just that we wanted to keep it as quiet as possible for the moment.'

'That the property isn't doing as well as it could?' she hazarded.

'Good lord, no!' His astonished ejaculation certainly put

paid to that line of thought, but it also left her as unaware as she had been before. 'With Chayne in control it's never been doing better.'

'Well—well ... what, then?' She spread her hands wide in confusion.

He looked at her as if considering the pros and cons of telling her and then shrugged. 'I guess it can't do any harm you knowing, but during the last couple of weeks some person or persons unknown have started helping us to cull our stock.'

For a time Rebel was no wiser than she had been previously. Then the penny dropped. 'You mean, someone's *stealing them*?' she gasped, astounded.

'Now you're getting the hang of it.'

Her steps slowed as she returned his glance questioningly. 'But why do you want it kept quiet? I'd have thought you would want it put abroad so they'd know you were on to them.'

'Uh-uh!' He shook his head in decisive negation. 'This way they still think they're home free and that we haven't wised up to them yet.'

'You're hoping to catch them red-handed?'

'That's about the size of it.'

'Have you any idea who it might be? You don't think it's a local, surely?'

His shoulders rose with deceptive indolence. 'We have our suspicions.'

As much as she would have liked to ask just who their suspicions had fallen upon, Rebel thought it best not to. Besides, she surmised Scott wouldn't have told her in any case. But she did spare a moment to wonder how on earth anyone would be foolhardy enough to deliberately take on the Cavanaghs. She didn't know how many there were in the family, of course, but the two she had met didn't exactly give the impression of being weak and unable to hold their own. In fact, they were the very last ones she would have chosen to set herself against if she had been one of the lawbreakers!

Having seen her to her room, Scott departed with a smile and a saluting finger raised to his temple, and closing the door behind her Rebel leant back against it, exhaling a contented breath. All in all, she had thoroughly enjoyed her first taste of absolute freedom, and although there had been a few disquieting moments where Chayne was concerned, she hoped that perhaps with practice she would soon feel as at ease and undisturbed in his company as she did with his less overpowering brother.

CHAPTER THREE

'WILL it fit?' Rebel asked anxiously as Murray prepared to heave her single piece of luggage into the back of the plane where, it seemed to her, there wasn't a spare inch of space to be found. It was already packed with a multitude of navy blue mail bags, paper-covered packages, cartons of all shapes and sizes, a stack of printed pamphlets, and goodness only knew what else!'

'Never fear! There, it's in!' Murray explained happily, and sent her a broad smile across the wing which separated them.

Rebel's mouth took on an extremely wry curve. The two rear seats of the small plane had obviously been removed to enable more goods to be carried, but even so she would never have credited the aircraft with being able to hold quite so much.

'Now, I suppose, the only question left to be asked is ... will it still be able to get off the ground?' she quipped, and not altogether facetiously.

'Of course it will!' he dismissed her fears blithely. 'What a little doubter you are!'

'Yes, well, it is the first time I've ever contemplated flying,' she tried to excuse her feelings of nervousness.

As he prepared to shut the door on the cargo area he sent

her a slightly incredulous look from beneath blond brows.
'Truly?'

She gave a succession of rapid little nods with her head.
'Mmm, honestly.'

He finished locking the door and came around the wing
to link her arm through his as they headed for the door on
the other side. 'Well, there's absolutely nothing to it,' he
attempted to reassure her amiably. 'You wait, I bet you'll
love it by the time we reach Pitereeka.'

'I hope so,' weakly.

'I know so,' she was corrected with confidence. 'There's
nothing quite like flying in one of these small aircraft.'

That Rebel was fully prepared to believe, but it wasn't
until they were actually airborne that she was willing to
say whether for good or bad. Once she could see how
relaxed and unworried Murray was at the controls, however, she discovered she was able to shed some of her
trepidation too and begin to derive some considerable
pleasure from the flight.

Above them the sky was a clear cobalt blue as far as the
eye could see, while below the ground spread away to a
hazy far distant horizon where glittering saltpans provided
a reminder of a one-time inland sea. From this height the
grass-covered plains and tree-lined gorges of the ranges immediately beneath them were clearly visible, as was the
occasional bright gleam of water from hidden rock pools or
strategically constructed earth tanks, and Rebel cast about
her interestedly for any further signs of human habitation.

'How many properties did you say we called at before
Pitereeka?' she called to Murray over the noise of the engine.

'Two. Irinka Plains and Winthunga.'

She returned to her study of the panorama below. 'How
long before we reach the first one? I can't see anything.'

'Don't be so anxious, it'll be another twenty minutes or
so yet,' he laughed at her eagerness. 'In any case, it will
come up on my side, not yours.'

A rueful nod and she tried to contain her increasingly
feverish sense of excitement. Today she was going to be

reunited with her brother after six long years and she could hardly bear these last few hours of waiting. It had been purgatory yesterday as she attempted to fill in time at the hotel, and if there hadn't been Ellen's friendly chatter at mealtimes she doubted if she would have spoken to another soul all day. Of the Cavanaghs there had been no sign, and she deduced they must have continued on their way south as had earlier been mentioned.

With a view to making the time pass more quickly she turned her attention back to Murray, asking, 'How many stations altogether will you call at today?'

'About thirty in all.'

Her winged brows lifted sharply. She hadn't realised it was that many! 'How do you locate them ... by compass reading?'

'I used to have to when I first started on the mail run,' he admitted with a grin of remembrance. 'But not these days. I find it easier by landmark now.'

Rebel nodded her acknowledgment, understanding how that could be the case. 'It must take you all day to finish, though,' she surmised.

He shrugged. 'If I don't waste any time en route I'll probably make it back to Deep Wells by about five-thirty or thereabouts.'

'What do you do for lunch?' she half laughed wryly. 'Eat while you go?'

'No, that's kindly provided by the Crawfords at Alajah.'

'And gladly too ... in return for the opportunity to see someone new and share the latest gossip, I've no doubt!'

Murray's blue eyes crinkled with laughter. 'Could be,' he assented lazily.

For a time Rebel went back to watching the ever-changing scenery below, then as she made an effort to peer past Murray for a glimpse of what she might be missing on the other side of the plane, happened to catch sight of the box of pamphlets behind him.

'Who wants that many brochures out here?' she questioned idly.

'Oh, they're not all for the one person,' he was quick to advise. 'They're for me to hand out as I go round. Some transport company's come up with a new air freight scheme they want to get the graziers interested in.'

'I see. You certainly have to be versatile for this job, don't you?' she chuckled. 'Now you're a sales rep as well as a pilot, a mailman, and a general carrier.'

'All part of the service,' he joked in return.

It seemed hardly any time after that and he was indicating towards his left where a cluster of buildings was becoming visible. 'There's Irinka Plains. Hold tight, and we'll be down before you know it.'

'Hold tight?' she repeated doubtfully. She didn't know if she liked the sound of that.

'That's right,' Murray verified calmly, beginning to ease back on the throttle. 'On the mail run I'm afraid we don't have time for the niceties of gentle, gradual turns. We bank once and come straight in.'

Frightened she might have been turning a pale shade of green, Rebel attempted to make light of it. 'Lovely!' she smiled from between clenched teeth. 'I just hope my stomach doesn't object to the manoeuvre, that's all!'

Murray flashed her a hasty glance. 'Why? You don't feel rotten, do you?'

'Not at present, no,' she was pleased to be able to report. 'But after what you've just told me there's no guarantee I'll stay that way.'

With a laugh he reached out and patted her encouragingly beneath the chin. 'Don't worry, little one, you'll be okay,' he advised cheerfully, and then, his concentration needed for other matters, returned his attention to the controls while Rebel held her breath and waited for the worst to happen.

It was just as well he had forewarned her of what to expect, she was to decide a few seconds later, because when Murray said he banked, he obviously meant *banked*, and if it hadn't been for her seatbelt Rebel was positive she would have found herself sitting hard up against the door

on his side of the plane! Their left wing just about disappeared from her sight as she stared at the ground through
his side window, and then, to her relief, they were levelling
out and racing towards the red dirt airstrip. Taxiing to a
halt, Murray sent her a teasing sideways glance.

'Well, that wasn't too bad, was it?' he quizzed.

Truthfully, she couldn't say it had been, and she shook
her head slowly from side to side, an answering smile pulling at her own soft lips. 'Not really.' She paused and then
chanced a full confession. 'In actual fact, now that I know
what's going to happen, I think next time I might find it
quite enjoyable.'

'That's the spirit!' he approved with a wink as he leant
across to open her door. 'Now, let's hop out and see if we
can't have old Angus's mail ready for him when he arrives,
otherwise he'll keep up here yarning for hours. It looks as
if he's on his way,' motioning over one shoulder to a cloud
of dust that was approaching from behind an obscuring
line of trees.

Once Murray had introduced her, and studiously kept
the rather talkative old man's mind on the job at hand,
Rebel found it was quite an education to watch the pro-
cedure necessary for others to receive their mail. Being a
private bag it was, of course, padlocked, and it took some
time for Angus to dig the requisite key from his pants'
pocket even before it could be opened and the mass of
letters and packages inside removed. This completed, he
then refilled the bag with all the station's outgoing mail and
relocked it before handing it back to Murray for eventual
transport back to the post office at Deep Wells. And while
he was returning the bag to the plane and taking out two
parcels and a carton of sundry items which had been
ordered for the property, Murray kept up a running com-
mentary on the daily happenings in town, interspersed
with the various benefits to be accrued from the proposed
new freight scheme.

'You know something?' Rebel remarked humorously as
soon as they had waved goodbye to the solitary figure

standing beside the Land Rover and were back in the air once more. 'I left out a title when I was describing your accomplishments before.'

'Oh, and what's that?' Murray enquired in wary amusement.

'Raconteur,' she supplied drily. 'After hearing all the information you managed to pass on during that short stop I bet they never have to read the newspaper! At least, not the local news, anyway.'

He shrugged self-effacingly. 'Ah, well, it can be a lonely life out here, and I always think it makes it more interesting to hear someone tell you what's been happening, rather than having to rely on reading it in a paper. More personal, more involving, somehow.'

Oh, yes, it would be that all right! She smiled across at him warmly. 'As I said, I don't doubt you're very welcome at the property where you have lunch.'

Half an hour later the whole process was repeated again at Winthunga and then it was time for them to alter their heading from north-east to due north for Rebel's long-awaited reunion at Pitereeka. This was the longest stretch they had undertaken so far—the longest Murray would take all day, in fact—and it was impossible for her to keep her eagerness for the journey to be completed from showing. Finally, when for the second time she had hinted that a little more speed wouldn't go amiss, Murray gave a disbelieving shake of his head.

'For heaven's sake, Rebel, simmer down, will you!' he ordered ruefully. 'It's like sitting next to a bubbling pot! We're making good time, and if we get there too early he probably won't even be out of bed when you arrive.'

'I wouldn't care if he wasn't,' she returned immediately, cheerfully unconcerned by his half-hearted stricture. 'I've waited too long for this moment to be worried by such incidentals. Can't you understand that, Murray?' She sought his appreciation of her position a trifle wistfully.

'Sure I can, little one,' he conceded, sighing. 'And I'm sorry if I seem to be trying to put a damper on your enthusiasm. It's just that it makes me nervous to see someone so overflowing with excitement as you are. People change a lot in six years, you know, and I'd hate to see that effervescence knocked out of you in a hurry.'

Although Rebel valued his solicitude, she couldn't share his sentiments, and especially not today of all days! She and Van had been so close as children, and even more so after their parents had died, that it was just inconceivable for her to imagine him not being as pleased to see her as she would be to see him. But for Murray's apparent peace of mind she was prepared to make concessions.

'Okay, for your sake, I promise to make an effort to restrain my natural ebullience until we reach Pitereeka.' A gleaming smile was directed his way as she proposed, 'A deal?'

A whimsical smile tugged at his lips. 'I could have hoped for more, for *your* sake, but if that's the best I'm going to get . . .'

'It is,' she inserted incorrigibly.

'Then I guess that's what I'll have to settle for.'

Strangely, his tone conveyed reluctance—the complete opposite of his words—but although Rebel frowned over it a little she was in no mood for deep analysis and, with a lightly dismissing shrug, she was soon back to watching the countryside skip past beneath them.

A voice suddenly crackling over the plane's radio served to bring her attention back inside the cabin again as she strove to make out what was being said, but when the accompanying static allowed her to only decipher the odd word—and as it obviously had nothing whatsoever to do with the mail plane, for the man beside her made no attempt to reply—she quickly lost interest and sought something else to keep her mind occupied.

'Where do you go once you leave Pitereeka?' was her first such effort.

'All over the place.' He reached down between their seats to retrieve a folded map he had wedged in there before they left Deep Wells and which he now handed to her. 'That'll show you better than I could explain,' he smiled.

Rebel's eyes roamed over the printed sheet interestedly. It was a detailed chart with every homestead in the area named and marked on it, as well as all the various towns, no matter how small. Murray's route, she saw, was drawn in red and it did indeed seem as if he would be going all over the place once he left their next stop. That heavily noted line zig-zagged purposefully from station to station until the whole page appeared a mass of red markings.

Not every property was listed for a visit by the mail plane, though, she was quick to realise. Mount Cavanagh wasn't—that had been one of the first names she had searched for—and she supposed the reason for their exclusion was the fact that they were close enough to a town not to warrant an air service.

'I see that you're also scheduled to make Pitereeka your last stop before returning to Deep Wells this afternoon. Why's that?' she pondered curiously.

'Very briefly, so the mail I pick up today can be sorted,' he explained.

'Isn't that done at Deep Wells?'

'Not all of it. You see, some will be local mail—that is, for Pitereeka, Castlefield, or places like that—and that can be delivered by road. There's not much point in my taking it all back to Deep Wells and then having to bring half of it out again on my next trip.'

'It would be rather a waste of time and space, wouldn't it?' Rebel nodded her comprehension. 'But what do you do while you're waiting for the sorting to be finished? Cool your heels out at the airstrip?'

'No, I usually make my way to the hotel for something cold,' he laughed. 'Most days I'm about ready for a drink by then.'

'Beer?' Two doubtful creases appeared between her finely marked brows. Surely drinking and flying was even less of a proposition than drinking and driving!

'Oh, brother! You really have got a lot to learn regarding the outback, haven't you?' Murray's eyes rolled skywards in disbelief.

Rebel's frown grew deeper. 'Why, what did I say wrong?'

'In order to answer that, I think perhaps I'd better let you in on some of the facts of life,' he retorted wryly.

'I already know those, thank you,' facetiously.

'I meant, life as it's lived out here,' he emphasised each word distinctly, ruefully.

'Oh, well, in that case ... go right ahead,' she invited in a teasing tone.

'I will!' He accepted her at her word. 'For a start, I don't know just what you've been envisaging Pitereeka to be like, but one thing I can assure you, it's not a bustling market plaza.'

Not even in her imagination had Rebel really gone so far as to suppose it was, but she decided against interrupting in order to inform him of that fact.

'To be quite honest, it's nothing more than a one-horse town set in the middle of nowhere, and with very little offering in the way of entertainment ... unless you happen to have a fancy for the occasional brawl,' he relayed ironically. 'It has a two-roomed post office, a one-roomed primary school, an hotel, a store, a bush hospital in charge of a nursing Sister—there isn't even a resident doctor— a School of Arts, which you will find is just another name for a hall where meetings can be held, and half a dozen assorted houses.'

If he had thought to shock her, he hadn't succeeded. It was more or less what she had expected. 'Okay, so it's not an inland paradise,' she shrugged nonchalantly. 'I still don't know what I said wrong.'

'Don't rush, I'm getting to that,' he countered smoothly. 'Now ... keeping in mind just how limited the facilities are in Pitereeka, who do you suppose is most likely to be equipped with a refrigeration plant, hmm?'

Rebel's grimace was ruefully executed. 'The hotel.'

'Very good!' he applauded sardonically. 'And now, where

do you think any visitor would go to buy a cold drink—whether that be water, fruit juice, lemonade, or any other kind of drink you can mention—when they're in Pitereeka?'

'The hotel,' she surrendered with a laugh. 'And I apologise for jumping to conclusions. I guess my own common sense should have warned me.'

'No harm done, you weren't to know,' he discounted her apology with a reciprocating smile. 'But I figured it was time someone put you wise to what the place was really like.' He sent her a speculating sideways look. 'Still as keen to arrive?'

'Oh, yes!' she nodded fervently.

'Then you'll be pleased to know it's just come into view.' He pointed towards what was, as yet, only a faint blur on the horizon. 'There! Can you see it?'

Rebel squinted eagerly into the distance. 'I'm not sure. I can see something that sort of looks like a break in the plains to the left of a high, sharp ridge.'

'That's it,' he confirmed. 'The ridge is Mount Cavanagh.'

So that was the Cavanaghs' home territory, she mused, and took a longer look this time. They were still too far away for her to be able to make out anything definite, though.

'Is the homestead visible from the air when we come in to land?' she asked in which she hoped was an impassive-sounding voice.

'No, it's way down the valley between Mount Cavanagh and the next ridge. You can only see it if you fly directly over it.'

She deliberated on this in silence and then, recalling her offer of same day service, thought it advisable to enquire, 'How far would it be from town?'

'By road? Oh, about thirty or forty miles would be my guess.'

'That far?' The distance hadn't looked particularly great on the map, and she said so.

'Mmm, but you're forgetting to take into account the contours of the land,' Murray pointed out logically. 'The road doesn't go straight over the top of the ridge, it winds around the base of it.'

'Is it a very good road? I mean, approximately how long would it take to get there?' Her questions were clearly arousing Murray's interest and, thinking he might have got the wrong idea as to why she was asking them, Rebel promptly flushed and rushed to explain, 'I'm trying to get the station's business for Van's store, and having rashly promised same day delivery without knowing the area I'd now like to know whether it is actually feasible.'

His curiosity fully kindled now, Murray's expression turned humorously quizzical. 'And just who did you promise this—er—delivery to?'

'Chayne.'

'That's who you discussed the whole idea with?' he sought further clarification once he had recovered from his initial look of surprise.

She nodded.

'And might I be permitted to ask what he had to say on the matter?'

For some unknown reason she sensed Murray was finding the situation very amusing and, in consequence, her reply was stiffly given. 'He said, more or less, that he would consider it.'

His lips twitched involuntarily. 'You must have been very persuasive.'

'I don't know quite what you mean by that, but if you're implying what I think you are, then I'll . . .'

'Hey, don't get me wrong!' he immediately broke in, attempting to soothe her obviously ruffled feelings. 'I wasn't having a shot at you, little one. Far from it.'

'In that case, might *I* now be permitted to ask just why you appear to find the matter so humorous?' she queried sardonically.

'Er—only because it came as such a surprise to learn you'd sounded Chayne out about it already.' He didn't bother to hold back his smile this time. 'You only found out your brother ran the store in the morning, yet by evening

—I gather that was when the discussion took place—you're out trying to drum up business for him.'

That first slight, but definite, hesitation created some doubts in Rebel's mind as to whether he was telling the truth or not, but when, after a few seconds of puzzling thought, she could think of no reason for him to lie, she inwardly shrugged away her reservations and returned his smile with a wry grin.

'Well, it seemed a pity to waste the opportunity,' she confessed with her hands spread expressively wide.

'Even though your brother may perhaps prefer to keep his business small?'

Rebel looked taken aback. 'With a town the size you've just described, surely if you didn't trade with as many of the surrounding properties as possible, your business wouldn't be small ... it would be just about non-existent!' she retorted.

'Mmm, you're probably right.' Hunching one shoulder casually, he indicated ahead of them once more. 'Look, you can see the town more clearly now.'

A lot more clearly, she found, and straight away was conscious of the return of that bubbling feeling of excitement in the pit of her stomach. Now it was possible to make out some of the buildings even, and she turned to her companion swiftly.

'Which one's the store?' she asked. 'Can you pick it out from here?'

'Uh-huh,' he drawled laconically, and half laughing at her impatience. 'You see the two places opposite each other at the end of the street? Well, the larger one on the right is the hotel, the one on the left is the store.'

'It doesn't look very big,' she commented thoughtfully.

'What were you expecting ... a department store?'

Sparing only enough time to send him a speaking glance, Rebel swung her gaze downwards again. 'Is that a house attached to the rear of it?'

'Yes, that's the storekeeper's residence all right.'

And that was where Van would be right at the moment!

No, she just as rapidly amended after taking a look at her watch, it was a little after nine, so he would probably be in the store by now. She hugged her arms about her midriff excitedly. He would be completely unsuspecting, and she was about to spring the surprise of his life on him!

They were beginning to lose height now and as they completed their turn and came in to land Rebel found herself staring straight towards the green, shrub-covered slopes of Mount Cavanagh and it jogged her memory.

'You never did get around to telling me whether the road out there was any good,' she reminded Murray on feeling the wheels touch down and their momentum begin to ease considerably.

At the end of the strip he turned and taxied the plane back towards the town. 'Yes, well, I think I'd be inclined to call it scenic rather than anything else,' he furnished finally, drily.

'In other words, it's lousy!' she interpreted with an uncaring chuckle. Right at present nothing could dampen her good spirits.

'But pretty,' he inserted irrepressibly. 'Although I must admit that it has been known to suffer wash-outs and the like.'

'Sounds positively delightful,' she quipped drolly. 'I'm beginning to think it isn't only to cut down on the long distances that everyone out here chooses to fly their own planes either! And talking about roads,' she continued before he had a chance to reply, and with a note of dismay entering her voice, 'it never occurred to me until now, but just how am I supposed to get to town from here?' She gazed wide-eyed across the mile or so of ground which separated the two.

'No worries, you can go back with Jocelyn and the mail,' he put her mind at ease as he helped her over the wing and down on to the ground.

'That's a relief,' she smiled gratefully. 'Who's Jocelyn?'

'Jocelyn Wymer, the postmistress. Here she comes now.'

Rebel swung around in time to see an old car of dubious capability bumping and rattling over the strip towards them. It was brought to a shuddering halt beside the plane and a very large woman in her mid-fifties alighted. Immediately she headed for the luggage compartment.

'Morning, Murray. You got much for us today?' he was greeted with an easily familiarity as she opened the back of the car and began pulling out more of those blue mail bags.

Murray, meanwhile, was offloading some of his. 'Morning, Jocelyn. There's a fair bit,' he returned in the same condensed fashion. 'What have you got for me?'

'Not much.' The last pile taken out, she watched as he started to reload them in the plane. 'You got a passenger too, I see.'

Still continuing with the exchange of mail, Murray made the necessary introductions as concisely as possible, but after her first taciturn acknowledgment the older woman's brows drew together in a frown.

'*Rebel* Hayward,' she repeated thoughtfully. 'With a name like that you'd have to be a relative of Vandal Hayward.'

'Yes, he's my brother,' Rebel laid claim to the family tie with eager pride.

Jocelyn eyed her consideringly for a couple of seconds. 'There is a slight resemblance, at that,' she allowed eventually. 'But I haven't heard him say anything about a sister arriving.'

'That's because he doesn't know yet,' Rebel revealed gaily, her eyes shining with happiness. 'It's been quite a few years since I saw him last and I wanted to surprise him.'

'You think that's wise?'

The dourly voiced question stripped some of Rebel's confidence away and left her feeling inexplicably unsure of herself. 'I—I don't know what you mean,' she stammered.

'Oh, take no notice of Jocelyn, she just hates surprises of any kind, that's all,' Murray advised with a short laugh as he lowered her case to the ground beside her. 'She likes to know exactly what's going to happen, and when, for every minute of the day.'

Rebel smiled her thanks for the action and released a shaky breath. 'I see,' she murmured faintly.

'You'll be wanting a lift into town, I suppose?' Jocelyn's next enquiry was made in a less daunting tone, much to the younger girl's relief.

'If you wouldn't mind,' deprecatorily.

'It doesn't trouble me, another couple of hundred yards isn't going to affect the old bus any.' A hand was slapped down on to the bonnet of the car which set it bouncing to a tune of assorted creaks and groans. 'You'd better toss her case into the back as well, then, Murray.'

This done, the exchange completed and the appropriate papers signed, Murray prepared to depart. 'I'll see you about four this afternoon,' he said to the postmistress as he ducked beneath one of the radio aerial wires, heading for the open cabin door.

'Right you are,' she responded as she regained her seat in the car, and Rebel turned to take her leave of the pilot.

'Thank you for putting up with me on the flight,' she half smiled nervously. Now that she was actually here she was reluctant to lose the only person she was at all familiar with. Even Van would be a stranger for a while.

As if sensing her edgy state the tall blond with the twinkling eyes put his arm reassuringly across her shoulders. 'You're welcome, little one, and don't look so worried, you'll be okay. I'll pop in and see how you're making out when I come back this afternoon, shall I?'

She accepted his offer gratefully. 'Thank you, I'd like that.'

'If you should—um—need some help at any time, though, keep Jocelyn in mind, hmm?' he counselled with sudden seriousness. 'She's a good listener and she's got a down-to-earth head on her shoulders.'

'I don't think I'd be game to ask,' Rebel laughed unsteadily. 'She's not exactly encouraging, is she?'

'Maybe not,' he couldn't do otherwise but agree. 'But don't let her manner put you off, she means well.'

A sound, somewhere between a cough and a long-suffering sigh, emanated from the subject of their discussion and Rebel took a hasty look over her shoulder.

'I believe I'm being told to get a move on,' she grimaced ruefully. 'So, thank you once again, and I'll see you this afternoon.'

'For sure, and ... good luck!'

The car was only half way to town before the mail plane was back in the air and Rebel watched it disappear into the brilliant blue sky with a feeling of regret. No matter how hard she tried she still couldn't quite recapture that inspiriting sense of excitement that had been so evident prior to their landing.

'You planning on staying long?' Jocelyn's also staccato enquiry brought her thoughts back to earth with a start.

'I—I don't know really,' she began uncomfortably, chewing at her lip. Up until that moment she hadn't really given it any consideration. All her thoughts had been concentrated upon finding Van as quickly as possible. 'I guess it will all depend.'

'It's not just a holiday you're on, then?'

'That's up to Van.' Her reply came a little faster this time, although she could have wished the other woman would stop picking flaws in her plans with such deadly accuracy.

'You expecting a welcome?'

Rebel's eyes widened in amazement as she swung her head to her right. 'Of course! Why shouldn't I?'

Jocelyn's lips pulled in at the corners and her solid shoulders rose in an indifferent shrug. 'You didn't answer either of his letters.'

'But—but how ...?' Surely Van hadn't told *everyone* in Pitereeka of her mistakenly believed remissness!

'I'm the postmistress, remember?' Jocelyn thankfully put that surmise to rest. 'He's only written two letters since he's been here—both to a Miss R. Hayward, somewhere in

Adelaide—and neither of which received a reply.'

'Only because I didn't receive them,' Rebel defended herself promptly, and a little resentfully at being interrogated by a total stranger. 'I can assure you I would have written if I'd known where he was.'

Brown eyes surveyed her swiftly but thoroughly. 'You seem to have found him easily enough ... now!' was the pointed charge.

First Scott and now this woman, Rebel fumed, and determined to set the record straight once and for all. 'Easily!' she echoed on a scornful note. 'It was certainly anything but that! It took me almost a year of selected advertising in the newspapers before anyone could even give me a clue as to his whereabouts, and even then the information was twelve months old. It was just fortunate for me that he hadn't moved too far from his last known address and that the station agent in Deep Wells could remember him buying the store here. But no, Mrs Wymer, my location of Van didn't come about *easily*!'

Surprisingly, Jocelyn was not only unperturbed by the outburst but a trifle amused as well. 'You can forget the Mrs, no one uses surnames in Pitereeka,' she informed the stiffly held figure next to her wryly. 'And I'm pleased to learn you're not as uncaring as it appeared, but ...' she paused, and to her passenger's even greater astonishment, there appeared to be laughter lurking in the depths of her eyes, 'do you mean people *do* actually answer those advertisements for missing persons?'

Glad to have rid herself of her resentment, and to have had her story accepted, Rebel now found herself able to relax, a little more. 'Not many,' she supplied drily. 'I only ever received the one, from a man named Eric Bevan who, apparently, was on the same shearing team as Van at one time.'

'*Eric Bevan!*' It was plain Jocelyn knew the name. 'Good lord, I would never have believed it! He never writes letters. He's a real loner, that one.'

'You know him? He's still in the area?' The questions

came rapidly. 'I did write to thank him for his information, but I'd rather do it in person if I could.'

The postmistress shook her head pessimistically. 'I know him, of course, but I haven't seen him in this district since . . . oh, about last March. Where'd you write to him at?'

'I can't remember offhand. It was one of those long unpronounceable names, you know? It started with a B, I think.'

'Doesn't sound like any place I know of around here,' the other woman disclosed after a moment's meditation. 'I guess he must have moved on, after all.'

They were approaching the town now and Rebel's interest was distracted from the conversation as her attention was caught elsewhere. It was exactly as Murray had described it, except that she hadn't envisaged the buildings being quite so widely spaced apart. They certainly didn't believe in living on top of one another, she observed whimsically.

The post office, she noticed as they passed, was located on the opposite side of the wide and dusty street to the store, as were the community hall and the hotel, but that was all she had time to see before Jocelyn was slowing outside the last low-roofed building.

Rebel stared at it half joyfully, half dubiously, for although the side of the sandstone structure had been a warm mellow gold in the clear morning light, the front—clothed as it was in shadows from the wide overhanging awning, and with its dust-laden windows shuttered, and the heavy wooden door bolted—presented anything but a welcoming picture. A nervous swallow and she turned to her companion with a forced smile on her lips.

'Thank you for the lift,' she murmured gratefully. Then, waving a hand towards the store, 'I guess Van must be a bit behind this morning. He hasn't opened up yet.'

Jocelyn looked as if she was about to make some comment, then shrugged and changed her mind. 'Yes, well, I'll get your bag for you,' was all she said in the finish.

Her hesitation did nothing to boost Rebel's fast declining confidence and eventually she was glad to wave the older woman goodbye as she prepared to make her presence known to her brother. Ever since her arrival in Pitereeka, Jocelyn Wymer had done nothing but create doubts in her mind!

CHAPTER FOUR

TAKING a deep breath, Rebel drew herself up to her full five feet six and, pulling open the rather battered and torn flyscreen, rapped decisively on the door behind it. When no one came to open it she began to wonder if perhaps she should go around to the back and try at the residence, but on thinking she might have caught the sound of someone inside the shop she decided to pound on the wooden obstruction one more time.

On this occasion she was relieved to note the reaction was almost immediate and as she heard the bolts being drawn back on the other side a delighted smile began to play about her mobile mouth at the thought of the reunion which was to take place so shortly. To her utter deflation, however, it wasn't a man who appeared in the dim opening as the door was pulled minimally ajar, but a girl some twelve months or so her junior.

A girl, moreover, who not only didn't seem pleased at the intrusion, but who didn't bother to hide it either as she took one hard look at Rebel and the suitcase beside her and announced in uncordial tones, 'The hotel's across the street.'

Mixed with Rebel's feeling of vexation—it would have been obvious to anyone with only half a brain that this wasn't the hotel—was one of dismay as she found herself wondering if Van could possibly be married, and this most inhospitable girl his wife! Oh, but she couldn't possibly be, she promptly went on to deny the likelihood of such a circumstance, otherwise someone would have mentioned it to her, surely! Having come to her conclusion she returned the fair-haired girl's discourteous stare impersonally.

'I don't want the hotel, thank you,' she rejected the supposition coolly. 'I came to see Vandal Hayward.' When the other girl showed no sign of moving, she continued with just a little asperity, 'He *is* here, isn't he?'

'Yeah, he's here,' came the admission at last, along with a suspicious narrowing of pale blue eyes. 'What's it to you?'

Rebel curbed her mounting impatience with difficulty. Just whose shop was it, anyway? 'I'd like to speak to him, if you don't mind,' she advised in as level a voice as possible.

'What about?'

'I don't consider that's any of your business!' Rebel's forbearance came to an abrupt halt. 'Now, are you going to tell him there's someone waiting to see him, or shall I go round the back and tell him myself?'

'He might not be ready to see anyone yet,' the hindering blonde began. But on seeing Rebel make a move towards her suitcase, she conceded sullenly, 'All right, all right! I'll see if he wants to speak to you.'

With a push that was obviously meant to slam the door, but which only resulted in it rebounding further open, the girl retreated into the darkened interior of the store and left Rebel waiting anxiously outside once more. In no way could it have been called an auspicious beginning, and just who the fair-haired girl was she had no idea, but helpful she definitely wasn't. For Van's sake, Rebel could only hope she wasn't employed to assist in the shop, because if this morning's effort was any indication of her normal attitude then it was a fair assumption that she turned away more custom than she encouraged.

Across the street, in the newly painted and surprisingly large hotel, two people could be heard breaking into sudden laughter, and the sound did a tremendous amount to revive Rebel's flagging spirits. Fortunately, it seemed, not everyone in Pitereeka was possessed of reserved and unaffable personalities. At least two persons were willing to share their enjoyment on such a beautiful day.

Inside the store the sounds didn't appear anywhere near as pleasant, and even from where she was standing Rebel could hear quite plainly every word that was said. The first derisive voice she knew immediately.

'There's some snooty redhead outside who says she wants to see you, Van.'

'Oh?' There was a quickening of interest in the tone, but Rebel couldn't quite say for certain yet that it was her brother speaking.

'Yeah, and when I asked her what about she said it was none of my business.'

The following quiet chuckle succeeded in arousing two distinct emotions. One of overwhelming excitement on Rebel's part—she would know Van's subdued laugh any time—and one of querulous accusation from the girl with him as she hissed, 'Who is she, Van? Who *is* she?'

'How the hell should I know until I've seen her!'

'Well, you must have some idea! Or have you known so many redheads that you can't decide which one it's most likely to be?' sarcastically.

'Oh, shut up, Sharon!' the voice was louder now, as if its owner was nearing the bead curtain which separated the store from the residence behind, but it was also weary and embittered too, Rebel noted sadly. Nothing at all like the lighthearted Van she used to know. 'Your family doesn't own me yet, you know!'

This last sent a deep frown descending on to Rebel's forehead as she attempted to figure out just exactly what he had meant by the remark, but when a figure shouldered its way through the curtain and came towards her all such thoughts fled as she stared through the intervening gloom at the form of her beloved older brother. Of course, if she hadn't previously heard him talking, and if the station agent hadn't prepared her for his beard, she might have been hard put to it to recognise him at all. He didn't seem as tall as she remembered—he was probably no more than four inches taller than she was—and he was certainly thinner than he had been. So much so, in fact, that she might have said almost to the stage of emaciation. His hair was much longer now too, and with that beard to hide most of his face from view, he looked a total stranger.

The remainder of his appearance wasn't altogether prepossessing either, she had to admit ruefully. His shirt and pants bore enough creases for him to have slept in them, his eyes definitely didn't have the glow of good health, his hair was dull and lifeless, and his beard could have done with a good trim. Summing it all up in one word, she could only have described him as looking extremely unkempt!

But none of that seemed to matter as he neared the doorway. 'Van?' she greeted him in a shaky, tentative manner.

'Yes?' His forehead furrowed and she could also see him trying to force recognition. 'Do I know ...?' All of a sudden he stopped as realisation came and he couldn't take his eyes off her as he exclaimed incredulously, 'Rebel! It is you, Reb, isn't it?'

Emotion filled her and all she could do was nod.

With a jubilant yell he swept her off her feet and whirled her around in his arms. 'Oh, Reb, it's so good to see you again! And there of all places! I never thought to see the day.'

'Nor did I,' she panted. It was difficult to breathe while he was squeezing her so tightly. 'I had the devil's own job tracking you down.'

At last he set her back on her feet. 'What do you mean, you tracked me down?' he puzzled. 'I wrote to you often enough telling you where I was.'

Conscious of the small group of interested spectators which his yell had brought forth on the opposite side of the street, as well as the surly blonde still hovering inquisitively in the background, Rebel lowered her voice a fraction. 'But I didn't get any of them, Van. You should know what Aunt Enid was like with mail.'

His mouth thinned angrily. 'You've never received even *one* letter from me since I've been gone?'

'Not one, I'm afraid,' sorrowfully.

'Oh, God, I could murder the callous pair of bastards!' he exploded fiercely. 'You must have thought me a nice type of dingo to skip and then not even bother to write to you.'

'No, of course I didn't!' she protested. 'I guessed what was happening even if I had no proof of it. But ...' her eyes slid to the group outside the hotel again, 'do you think we could discuss all this inside ... in private?' she pleaded embarrassedly.

'What?' He saw the direction her gaze was taking and smiled in understanding. 'Oh, yes, of course. Come on through. I'm sorry for the mess, but I—er—haven't been able to clean it for a while.'

'You've been sick?' she queried worriedly. He certainly didn't look well.

'That's the understatement of the year!' hooted the girl who was lolling insolently against the counter. 'He's usually so ...'

'Why don't you shut your mouth, Sharon, and clear out!' Van cut her off furiously.

'Without so much as an introduction to your ... *friend*?' she emphasised insinuatingly.

He let out a heavy breath and, as if he knew she would never leave without the information she wanted, ground out as briefly as possible, 'Sharon Lambert—my sister, Rebel.'

Neither girl responded to the introduction aloud, Rebel merely acknowledging it with a nod of her head, and Sharon not even going that far before she swaggered past them on her way to the door.

'Vandal and Rebel, hmm?' she pondered from the opening, and cast them a malicious glance. 'It doesn't sound as if your parents had very high hopes for either of you, does it?'

Van took a couple of steps forward, but the girl was gone before he had a chance to reach her and Rebel sighed with relief to see her go.

'What a perfectly objectionable specimen,' she grimaced. 'I hope she doesn't work for you.'

'No, thank heavens! She just hangs around making a nuisance of herself, and hoping for a chance to take over.'

'When you're ill?' She couldn't get it out of her head that his health wasn't as it should be.

'Not ill,' Van disclaimed with a light laugh as he led the way behind the counter, carrying her case. 'Off colour a bit, that's all.'

Rebel followed, her expression thoughtful. He hadn't really put her mind at ease, but she guessed now wasn't the time to press the matter either, so she kept silent. There would be plenty of time to come back to it later.

There wasn't much of an opportunity for her to look over the shop as she came through, but what did catch her eye didn't appear very promising. It was dark, musty, covered in a thick film of dust, and those items that were on the shelves seemed to have been tossed there in a haphazard fashion. Partially unpacked and unopened cartons made the floor area into something of an obstacle course, while the papers and magazines laid out on the counter didn't look as if they had been changed for months, and she could only hope that the residence at the back would show some improvement on what she had seen so far.

Depressingly, and disappointingly, it didn't, she discovered to her consternation on passing between the strands of the bead curtain. Here also were the same signs of neglect and indifference to creature comforts with clothes and belongings strewn indiscriminately from one room to another. As for the kitchen, she gave an involuntary shudder at first sight and decided that the less she thought about that the better.

'Here, have a seat while I make us some coffee,' Van invited, dragging a shirt and a towel from one of the chairs at the table and giving it a wipe with the towel before holding it out for her.

Rebel accepted it with a half smile and, trying to ignore

the food-encrusted plates spread over the table and sink, and the ants which had discovered some spilt honey on the plastic tablecloth, set about making mental plans as to how she was going to attack the cleaning of this place. One thing was for certain, she had no intention of remaining there with it in that condition!

Van filled an old kettle with water and set it on the gas stove, then collected the plates from the table and stacked them with the others of their kind in the sink. He gave the table a cursory wipe with a sponge that had seen better days—completely missing the honey and the ants—and, finding no clean mugs in the cupboard above the wooden dresser, grabbed a couple off the sink and began rinsing them out. Placing them on the table, still wet, he spooned out coffee from a jar and took a seat while he waited for the water to boil.

'Now, first of all, how long are you allowed to stay?' he asked eagerly. 'I'm surprised that miserable pair let you come at all, to be quite honest, and especially after them keeping my letters from you.'

'Yes, well ...' Rebel's lips twisted wryly. 'It wasn't so much them *letting* me come as it was them telling me not to bother coming back if I left.'

He snorted in disgust. 'That would be about par for them! I guess I should have expected as much.' Gradually his expression began to lighten. 'Does that mean, then, that you're free to stay as long as you like? That there's no special reason for you returning to Adelaide?' he probed swiftly.

'No, there's no special reason for me to return and, yes, I'm free to stay for as long as you'll have me,' she smiled.

'For as long as I'll ... Are you nuts? That'll be for good!' He reached across the table to grasp her hand elatedly. 'God, you've just given me my best news ever! That's fantastic, Reb! You'll never know how much I've wanted this to happen. Everything I did in the early days was aimed at getting some money behind me just so the two of us could be a family again.'

Touched by his devotion, unbidden tears started into Rebel's eyes. 'It must have been a great disappointment to you, then, when you believed I couldn't even be bothered to write to you.'

'Initially, I put it down to you being five years younger than I was. You were still only a kid, after all.' Van was able to shrug it off unconcernedly now. 'I did let it get to me this last year or so, I'm afraid, and I know I've let things get away from me a bit.' He glanced around the room as if really seeing it for the first time in a long while and his demeanour was apologetic. 'But I'll make it up to you, you'll see. Everything will be different now.'

'You don't have to make anything up to me, Van,' she protested. 'It's enough that you're providing me with a roof over my head.'

'For the moment, anyway.' He ran his fingertips worriedly over his forehead.

'Meaning?'

The shrill scream of the kettle demanded attention and his reply had to wait until he had filled their mugs. Afterwards, he regained his seat heavily and kept his eyes averted as he stirred sugar into his drink.

'I suppose I may as well let you know the worst, because if I don't, someone else will,' he sighed, and sent her an abject look.

Concerned over the turn the conversation was taking, Rebel concealed her trepidation as best she could beneath an encouraging smile and waited for him to continue.

'As I said, about a year back I started to allow what I wrongly believed was your defection to rattle me. Oh, I know I should have had more faith—as you did—but I'm sorry, I didn't. I began drinking, heavily, in my bout of self-pity,' he admitted in a monotone. 'The result was I lost the job I had at the time, but in a moment of what was becoming increasingly rare straight thinking, I decided to buy the store here before I managed to drink every last cent of my savings away. Unfortunately, though, that didn't put an end to it. With the hotel right across the street it was all too easy to slip over there for a quick one. Except it never seemed to stop at that, and more often than not I was the last person out when they closed trading for the day. It was handy too with the ready cash coming into the store. That was, until it came time for me to re-order and there wasn't any money to pay the invoices.'

He took a mouthful of his coffee and, as he stared un-seeingly at the mug he replaced on the table, his lips curled with bitter self-mockery. 'So that was when I came up with the idea that I'd be able to recoup all I'd lost if I tried my hand at a few games of cards . . . for big stakes.'

Rebel couldn't suppress a sharp inhalation, beginning to suspect what was coming, and waited apprehensively for his next disclosure.

'I'd always been pretty lucky before when I'd played in small games, but . . .' Van uttered a short mirthless laugh, 'somehow it isn't the same when winning means so much to you. Maybe it alters the way you play, or something, but whatever it is, I sure didn't have any luck when I needed it. Within a couple of months I was so deeply in debt there was only one course left open to me. I took out a loan against the store,' he concluded dejectedly.

'From the Lamberts?'

Van's head jerked upwards rapidly, his eyes showing his disbelief. 'How in hell did you know that?'

She shrugged one shoulder deprecatorily. 'I'm sorry, but when I was waiting for Sharon to tell you I was here I heard you say something to the effect that her family didn't own you *yet*. So, putting two and two together . . .' There was no need for her to complete the sentence.

'Yes, well, that's about how things stand at the moment. Not a very pleasant situation for you to walk into, eh?' contritely.

'Not quite what I was expecting, that's for certain,' she smiled in an effort to jolly him out of the depressed mood he had fallen into during his narration. 'But if we both put our minds to it and watch what we spend'—she had become an expert at that after living with Aunt Enid and Uncle

Roger for so long!—'we should be able to get the place back on its feet and have that loan repaid before too long. How much was it for, anyway?'

When he told her the amount Rebel was in danger of joining her brother in his despondent state. That large an amount she just hadn't anticipated!

'What sort of repayment terms have they stipulated?'

'I don't think they—er—expected me to make any,' he confessed with obviously painful honesty.

'You mean you haven't signed a legal form? There's no time limit been set on it?'

'I'm not sure. I know I did sign something.' He shook his head despairingly. 'I'm sorry, Reb, I've made a complete hash of it, haven't I?'

'Of course you haven't,' she retorted bracingly. 'We'll just have to manage with what we've got for the moment, that's all. Unless, of course ...' she paused and her brows rose quizzically, hopefully. 'I don't suppose you happen to have any money left from that loan, do you?'

'Only a little. Most of it went to pay debts. Although I did use some of it to buy more stock for the store,' he added a little more brightly.

The obstacles on the floor, Rebel recalled ruefully. 'Well then, we're on our way already,' she smiled. 'All we have to do now is to clean the place up and make it presentable and we'll have that loan repaid before you know it,' adding a silently prayed, 'I hope!' for her own reassurance.

'And I guess the first place we'd better get ready is a room for you to sleep in,' Van suggested helpfully.

Rebel shook her head gently and chose her words carefully, not wanting to hurt his feelings. 'I think it might be best if we start in here,' she laughed, but very aware all the same of the ants' scouts which were now nearing the sugar. If they weren't halted soon they would be through every cupboard as well. 'By the look of the dresser you're just about out of plates, and we'll be needing those before I need a bed.'

He looked about him remorsefully. 'Until now there

didn't seem much reason to care what sort of a mess the place was in.'

'Well, there is now,' she reminded him cheerfully, jumping to her feet. 'And the sooner we get started, the sooner we'll be finished. I'll just change into something a little more workmanlike and then I'll be right back.'

The room where Van had deposited her suitcase was as untidy as the rest of the house, but Rebel paid scant heed to it as she donned a pair of old jeans and a sleeveless cotton shirt in place of the matching slacks and top she had worn on the plane. In minutes she was back in the kitchen where she found Van beginning to run hot water into the sink.

'That's nice furniture back there,' she remarked conversationally as she joined him at the sink and reappraised the kitchen. 'In fact, it's all quite nice. Oldish, but nice, all the same. Did you buy it, or did it come with the house?'

'It came with the house. The previous owners were retiring to the coast, so they sold it along with the store because they figured it would cost less to replace it all in Adelaide than it would to freight this to where they were going.'

'Their loss, your gain,' she grinned.

'Something like that,' he agreed, and caught her to him in a convulsive bear-hug. 'God, it's good to have you here, Reb! Or have I already told you that?'

'I think so,' she returned a little mistily. 'Although it's not a sentiment I'm likely to get tired of hearing.'

'Which is probably just as well, since I've the feeling you're going to be hearing it said repeatedly over the next few weeks.'

'You think the novelty of my being here will have worn off by then, do you?' she teased in assumed indignation.

'Never,' he contradicted in all seriousness before turning her loose and facing her towards the sink. Whereupon he grinned facetiously. 'And especially if you keep doing my washing up for me!'

'For that you can clean out all the cupboards,' she ordered in the same light vein. 'It wouldn't surprise me if

half of them haven't seen the light of day for goodness
knows how many months, and by now just about anything
could have made their home in there.'

Van swept her an exaggerated bow. 'I'm yours to command, my dear sister.'

With both of them working hard it wasn't long before
the room was shining clean from top to bottom and, feeling
happier to see it so, Rebel began her assault on the rest of
the house. By lunch time she had collected every article of
dirty clothing she could find, washed them, and had them
hanging on the line to dry—a process which would be
accomplished extremely quickly, she had decided, on feeling the sting of the summer sun while pegging them out.
Her bedroom was now spick and span too—with all her
clothes put neatly away—as were Van's bedroom and the
bathroom.

'If we get stuck into the rest of the rooms this afternoon,
we can start on the shop tomorrow,' she suggested as they
were taking a well earned break with their lunch. 'From the
look of it, I rather think it will take a whole day to get that
back into anything even approaching a semblance of order.'

'More than likely,' Van smiled faintly, indifferently almost, and causing Rebel to eye him with a mounting sense
of disquiet.

His enthusiasm had shown definite signs of waning during the last hour, she remembered. Even white teeth worried at her lower lip for a moment or two, and then she
elected to take the bull by the horns. She would get nowhere by avoiding the issue.

'Is something wrong?' she asked quietly.

'What makes you ask?' Van looked at her enquiringly.

'You seem to have lost some of your interest for the
project.'

'Have I?' he countered with a laugh. It sounded a trifle
forced to her. 'Maybe it's just been too much of a shock to
my system.'

'Well, you don't have to help with the cleaning if you'd
rather not,' she hastened to impress on him earnestly. 'I

don't mind doing it on my own if there's something else you'd prefer to do.'

A tinkle drifted down the passage towards them and Van was on his feet immediately. 'There's someone in the store,' he explained unnecessarily, since that was the second time someone had rung the counter bell that morning, and had disappeared in that direction before Rebel could say another word.

Saved by the bell! Her lips curved wryly and, extracting a cigarette from the packet on the table, she lit it, and drew on it thoughtfully. Although she considered she had the capability and the willingness to return the store to a paying proposition, at the same time she didn't want her brother to feel that she was attempting to usurp his position. He might have been the one to let it slide downhill, but he was still the owner, and perhaps she had unintentionally been forcing him into doing what she wanted. It might be more diplomatic, from now on, if she let him make the decisions with regard to what needed to be done.

'Someone wanting petrol,' Van relayed on his return. The store also doubled as the only service station in town with its solitary pump standing a short distance from the shop entrance. He headed for the fridge. 'I think I'll have a drink. How about you?'

'Yes, I think I might, that tea I made has left a distinctly metallic taste in my mouth.' She pulled an expressive face. 'I'll have passionfruit, please.'

'Mmm, the tea wasn't so good, was it?' he grinned commiseratingly. 'But I'm afraid that was my fault. I didn't explain about the taps,' indicating the three above the sink. 'The two on the left are hot and cold bore water, the one on the right is drinking water. That's connected to the rain tanks.'

Rebel nodded her comprehension slowly, ruefully. 'That could explain it. I'll make sure I don't do that again! Thank you,' she acknowledged as he scooted a can across the table towards her.

Van turned back to the fridge and retrieved a drink for

himself. 'Do you mind?' he ventured somewhat defensively, and holding up a can of beer for her inspection.

'Oh, hell, I don't expect you to ask my permission!' Her protest was helplessly made. 'I'm not here to sit in judgment, and—and I'm sorry if I've led you to believe otherwise by my pushy behaviour this morning. How about I keep my mouth shut from here on in and let you run things, hmm?'

Returning to his seat, he pulled the tab back on the can and took a long swallow. 'Apart from the fact that I didn't do a real good job of running things when I had the chance,' he began drily, 'I have no objections to you having a go with the store if you'd like to, believe me. Somehow I don't think I'm cut out to be a shopkeeper.'

'I must say that thought did occur to me too when I first heard you'd bought the place,' she admitted with a grin, and relieved that she hadn't upset him by her attitude. 'But if you're not interested in the store, what would you like to do?'

Van ran a finger meditatively down the side of his can wiping away the beads of condensation. 'Well ... as we do have the fuel franchise here in town, and as the work I think I most enjoyed since leaving Adelaide was the two years I spent in a truck workshop, I've sometimes thought I wouldn't mind giving it a go to see if I couldn't build up a sort of automotive repair shop,' he disclosed diffidently as he glanced across to gauge her reaction. 'There's a surprising amount of machinery in the district, apart from cars, and although a couple of the larger stations employ their own mechanics, mostly it seems to be a case of fix it yourself as best you can, or else take it into Deep Wells for repair.' He stopped and sent her a hopeful look. 'What do you think?'

'It sounds practicable,' she admitted tentatively. 'But wouldn't you need to outlay a lot of capital to set up something like that? You know, for equipment and so forth?'

'I don't think so, at least not to start with.' A perceptible eagerness was creeping into his voice. 'I already have quite a

collection of my own tools, and there was a stack of assorted
car parts, etcetera, left in the shed out the back when I
bought the store. I'd only want to start off small, in any
case, just to see how it goes.'

'I suppose we could always give it a try,' she allowed
with an easygoing hunching of her shoulders. 'If we don't
need a big outlay then we really won't have much to lose,
and if it should prove successful—who knows?—we may be
able to pay off the loan on the store twice as quickly.' A
deciding factor in her consideration.

'You wouldn't mind being left to manage the store on
your own?'

'I'd love it!' she grinned. 'More importantly, though, are
you really certain you'd be happy doing the other?'

He gave the question his deep concentration for a few
minutes. 'I think so,' he finally affirmed. 'I do like working
on engines, and although I may not have a very good record
so far for consistency with any one occupation, that was
really only because there wasn't any necessity for it. I just
knew I preferred the bush to the city and thought that if I
tried enough jobs I might eventually find my own little
niche out here somewhere along the way.'

'The store being your latest attempt?' half humorously.
Van had already given her a rundown on the others he had
tried, including those she had previously known about.

'And probably the least successful,' he conceded, smiling
contritely. 'Having to decide such things as whether to
order strawberry or raspberry jam just isn't in my line,
I'm afraid.'

'Well, you won't have to worry about that any more, it's
my province now. In the meantime, however ...' Rebel
took one last puff of her cigarette, stubbed it out in a large
glass ashtray and, rising to her feet, drained her can of
drink, 'there's work to be finished in here before I can even
start to think about what needs attention in the shop, and
it's not going to get done if I sit around the kitchen all
afternoon.'

Van emptied his own can and disposed of them both in

the waste bin. 'I'll get started in one of the other rooms, shall I?'

There was a teasing light in her vivid blue eyes as she eyed him consideringly. 'Are you positive there isn't something else you would rather be doing?'

'Not until I've helped you with the cleaning.'

'But you ...'

He held up a silencing hand. '*You* might not mind if I didn't help, Reb, but I would,' he advised soberly. 'It wasn't so much my enthusiasm that was waning before lunch as it was my self-disgust increasing at seeing you having to work so hard clearing up the mess I'd damned well made! It wasn't how I'd always pictured our reunion at all.'

'Oh, Van!' She threw her arms around him impulsively. 'It doesn't matter to me who does what, so long as what's left of our family is together again. That's what's important.'

'So is my helping you with this ... to me.'

He was in deadly earnest, and on noting the stubborn look about his mouth Rebel sighed and began to laugh. 'Okay, if that's the way you want it. You can start in the lounge while I wash these,' gesturing towards the plates they had used for lunch.

For three hours they continued toiling amid the afternoon's climbing temperature until the last specks of dust and dirt had been banished from within the house, and it was a concerted sigh of thankfulness they both uttered when at last they were satisfied each room was as spotless as they could make it.

'I don't know about you, but me, I'm for a shower,' Van declared, flexing his shoulders tiredly as they surveyed their handiwork.

'Me too,' smiled Rebel, and pulled at her damp shirt. 'Then I'll have to get that washing in and see about tackling the ironing.'

'Oh, give it away for today, Reb,' he urged anxiously. 'You've done enough without ploughing through that lot.'

'But I'd rather get it done before dinner because I'd like

to go over the paperwork for the store this evening if I could. See who to order from, what type of goods, the quantities, etcetera.'

'You sure don't mean to let any grass grow under your feet, do you?'

'Can't afford to,' she grinned. 'I want to be able to present some prices to Mount Cavanagh Station as soon as I possibly can.'

Van couldn't have looked more astounded if he'd tried. 'And just what do *you* know about Mount Cavanagh?'

'Only that, at the moment, they happen to purchase their supplies in Deep Wells, and that that's a practice I hope to alter in the very near future.'

'Some hope!' wryly.

'Oh?' She looked at him askance. 'Why's that?'

'Because that happens to have been where I was working as a stockman, and if you'll recall, I told you I lost that job due to my—er—slightly excessive habits.'

'You worked on Mount Cavanagh!' she repeated with a stunned expression. Now why hadn't Chayne mentioned that? 'And you were fired?'

He nodded regretfully. 'Yes, to both questions.'

'Then why would he have implied that it had been your own decision ... because you hadn't taken a liking to the work?' she quizzed musingly, and more to herself than to him.

'Who, Murray?' He shrugged. 'Probably because he either didn't know all the facts, or else he was ...'

'No, not Murray ... Chayne!' she interrupted to enlighten him, but with a perplexed frown still furrowing her forehead. 'And he said most of his knowledge of you was hearsay only,' on an accusing note.

'So it would have been since I left the station. I doubt if I've seen him more than twice since. But how in blazes do you know Chayne, anyway?' Van's astonishment was back at full strength.

'Oh, I met him and Scott in Deep Wells when I was arranging with Murray to bring me out here.' Her information was relayed casually, most of her thoughts continuing to be occupied elsewhere. 'But I still don't see why ...'

'Well, just because you've met them I shouldn't get my hopes up too high regarding the likelihood of them giving you their custom, if I were you,' it was his turn to break in this time, repressively. 'They're heavyweights in the grazing fraternity, and although they may all be very pleasant and easygoing socially, when it comes to business they're as farsighted and hardheaded as anyone you're likely to find. Apart from which, unfortunately for you, I don't happen to be held in their highest esteem right at present,' he concluded apologetically.

'Chayne said he would consider it if I could present him with comparable prices. Don't you think he meant it?'

Van moved his head in an incredulous gesture. It was clear he was finding it difficult to take it all in. 'You mean, you've already spoken to him about it?'

'Certainly!'

'And just how would that come into the conversation while you were arranging your flight with Murray?'

'It didn't,' she laughed at his obvious confusion. 'It was during the party at the hotel later that evening.'

He expelled a relieved breath at having sorted that out at least. 'And you say Chayne reckoned he would consider purchasing his supplies from here,' he now queried, but with his expression still a little unbelieving.

'More or less,' she confirmed, then reiterated her previous question. 'Don't you think he meant it?'

'If he said it, I would have to presume he meant it. As I have reason to know, Chayne Cavanagh is a man of his word,' he divulged drily.

'Meaning?' Though she suspected she knew the answer already.

'That while I was working for him I got one warning, and one only. Either pull myself together or I was out! Within two weeks I was out,' he sighed.

Rebel gazed up at him speculatively. 'You don't seem to

bear him any hard feelings because of it, though.'

'Why should I?' he countered fairly. 'He had every right to protect his property—even when perfectly sober I'm afraid I'm not a particularly good stockman—and besides, he wasn't entirely wrong in telling you I hadn't exactly taken a liking for the work,' he grinned. 'All those hours spent on horses or motorbikes mustering sheep and cattle, then dipping them, drenching them, and goodness knows what else, just wasn't for me. I soon discovered it only looks romantic and easy from a distance. Close to, it's un-adulterated hard work!'

'Like shearing?' she chuckled. He hadn't really enthused over that occupation either when they'd spoken of it earlier.

His ensuing grimace was very expressive. 'As far as I'm concerned, the only thing shearing's got going for it is the fact that once you learn the ropes, and if you really make an effort, you can earn pretty good money at it. It also has the advantage that with a lot of the properties being so far away from anywhere it's easy to save most of what you're paid. But I don't think I'll ever forget the pain in my back after my first day.' Wincing, even now, he stretched his back in recollection. 'I really thought I was crippled for life and would never stand upright again.'

'Yet you stuck at it for just on two years.' She had to admire his tenacity of purpose.

'Well, of course, you do—*eventually*—become conditioned to it, and as I said, it did enable me to save money, which was a very important factor at the time.'

'Then you decided a stockman's life just had to be easier.'

'Something like that.' His assent was ironically given. 'I figured I was financial enough by then not to have to worry about doing another season, so I thought I'd give that a go for a while. As it turned out, I'd probably have been better off if I'd stuck to shearing!'

'Except that it's doubtful if I would have found you if you had, what with you keep moving from station to station all the time.'

'Mmm, there is that, isn't there? It's nice to know *some*

good did eventuate from the unholy mess I've made of the last twelve months,' he derided himself in a mocking tone.

'Oh, don't be a fool,' she chided fondly. 'Everyone's entitled to make some mistakes and, in any case, that's all behind us now. The future is all that counts from here, and that I refuse to even contemplate as being anything but a wholehearted success!'

Van linked his arm with hers and together they began heading for the passage. 'You sure are brimming with confidence and optimism, aren't you?' he teased.

In return Rebel sent him a look filled with wry laughter. 'Weren't you too, when you first escaped our dear relatives' restrictive household?'

'It is rather like throwing off the shackles of bondage and rejoining the ranks of the free, isn't it?' he concurred with feeling.

She couldn't have put it better!

CHAPTER FIVE

FEELING refreshed, although not necessarily cooler after a shower wherein the temperature of the cold water varied little from the hot, Rebel was ironing on the enclosed back verandah when Van emerged from the bathroom. For a time she could only stare at him in pleased surprise as she took in his changed appearance.

Gone was the straggly beard which had made him look such a stranger, and in its place an expanse of decidedly paler skin than that which covered the upper half of his face. His clothes were also a great improvement. Pale blue short-sleeved shirt and darker blue denims, both clean and unwrinkled, were a welcome contrast after the rumpled outfit he had been wearing all day.

'Well, I hope my shower and change did as much for me as yours did for you,' she quipped lightly.

He gave a sheepish smile and put a hand to his still damp hair. 'I thought I might take a walk up the street and see if Lloyd—Jocelyn's husband—feels like doing a spot of hair cutting. He's a dab hand with a pair of scissors and I reckon I'm about due.'

Understatement! she grimaced to herself. But to him, and not wanting to make him feel any more abashed than he obviously did already, she merely nodded aquiescently. 'Okay. I'll see you when you get back.'

'I don't expect I'll be gone all that long.' He spoke reassuringly.

'That's all right, I've got plenty to occupy me. Before you go, though ...' she called after him as a thought occurred to her, and he turned back enquiringly. 'What time do you usually have dinner?'

'More often than not, I don't, so whatever time suits you will be quite acceptable to me.'

No wonder she'd thought he didn't look very well! 'Some time between six-thirty and seven, then?' she suggested.

'Sounds great,' he owned with a grin and continued on his way to the door.

It took a while for Rebel to finish the ironing. He must have just about been down to his last set of clean clothes, she decided ruefully. But it did finally come to an end and she carried the pile through to his room with a thankful sigh.

She had only just placed them on his dresser when the bell rang in the store and she hurried eagerly into the hall. This would be the first time she had attended to a customer, and she was looking forward to it. Pushing through the bead curtain, she came to a halt on seeing who was standing on the other side of the counter and a wide welcoming smile lit her attractive face.

'Murray! Is it really that time already?' She glanced at her watch to check for herself and found it was even later than four, it was half past. 'Heavens, but today's disappeared quickly. Would you like to come through and have a drink?'

'No, thanks, little one, I've just had one over at the pub. I only called in to see how you were making out before I made my way back to the post office.'

Rebel deliberately schooled her features into a less joyful expression. 'If you mean with regard to Van, then I don't really think I ought to even discuss it with you.'

'Why? What did I do?' He looked as bewildered as he sounded.

'It's what you *didn't* do!' she retorted.

'Eh?'

'You might at least have given me a warning what to expect!' she at last saw fit to elucidate in her most reproachful manner. 'You knew about his drinking, didn't you? All three of you did! That's what you ... and Chayne!' now she came to think about it, 'were meaning when you said I should be prepared for any changes, wasn't it?'

He lifted one shoulder excusingly, pacifying. 'I—we didn't want to spoil your reunion for you, little one, by making you worry before you even got here. We figured you'd find out soon enough.'

'I still think you could have dropped bigger hints,' she charged dolefully. 'Sometimes it helps to be prepared, you know.'

'But not necessarily in this instance,' he asserted with an engaging smile. 'You seem to have worked wonders already without any preparation. I hardly recognised him when I went in for my drink a while back.'

'You mean he's in the hotel?' she gasped, her eyes clouding with dismay. That was completely different from his having a drink at home, like lunch time.

'Only to celebrate your arrival and to prove to all the disbelievers that you weren't a figment of his imagination,' he hastened to assure her.

'But he said things would be different from now on,' she cried disappointedly. 'He as good as promised!'

Murray reached across the counter and grasped her by the shoulders. 'Listen, little one, habits are often harder to break that we'd like them to be, so don't go expecting too many miracles, too soon. Hell, the change you've wrought this far should be enough to satisfy you for one day,' he counselled encouragingly. 'Sure, he's having a couple of drinks to celebrate, but in case you don't know it yet, that's something quite different from drinking just for the sake of it!' He smiled gently into her troubled face. 'Whatever you do, Rebel, don't try and tie him up too tightly. Taut ropes are inclined to break, those with some play left in them don't.'

'I don't want to tie him up, Murray, I just don't want him to lapse into the same mistakes again, that's all,' she tried to defend herself, albeit a trifle tearfully.

'And if you want my honest opinion, I don't think he will ... now that you're here.'

She stared up at him hopefully, wanting to be convinced. 'Don't you really?'

'I just said so, didn't I?' he smiled banteringly, releasing her.

Rebel combed her fingers through her hair in a vague gesture, still uncertain. 'Don't you think I should say anything to him, then?'

'Well ...' His lips pursed contemplatively and then he shrugged. 'I think I'd at least wait and hear what he has to say first, and then play it by ear, if I were you.'

'Okay, I'll give it a try your way,' she sighed, and smiled faintly. She didn't really have much choice, she had no experience of her own to call on. 'And I'm sorry for involving you in my problems. What was your day like?' she went on in an attempt to change the subject.

'Much the same as usual,' he laughed. 'Periods of silence in the air, interspersed with spells of rapid conversation on the ground.'

Her answering smile removed the last traces of worry. 'And how often do you do the trip, just the once each week?'

'No, twice,' he corrected. 'Mondays and Thursdays.'

'So we won't be seeing you again until next week now?'

'Uh-uh, tomorrow night, as a matter of fact,' he grinned at having to amend yet another of her suppositions. 'The local Christmas dance and party is being held over at the hall. Everyone will be there from miles around.'

'Even from as far as Deep Wells?'

'Further in some cases. As I told you this morning, for most of the year there isn't much on in the way of entertainment out here, so when there is ...'

'No one forgoes the opportunity to participate,' Rebel supplied wryly for herself.

'Just about,' he endorsed. 'Although it will probably be a good chance for you to meet everyone in the district too.'

'En masse?' Her slim eyebrows shot upwards explicitly. 'I shall never remember who's who!'

'Maybe not, but at least it will make people aware of your presence.'

'Is that important?'

'It could be if you want to put this store back on its feet. Which I presume you do.'

'Yes, of course I do, but ...'

'It will let everyone know that it isn't just Van they'll be dealing with any more—who, unfortunately, didn't exactly gain a reputation for reliability—but that there's now someone else here who's only too anxious to cater to their needs,' he explained.

'Oh, I see,' she nodded. 'You mean, it's like letting them know it's under new management, that sort of thing?'

'More or less.' He sent her a roguish look from narrowed eyes. 'Of course, it probably wouldn't do your cause any harm either if you could bring to bear—on the men, anyway—a few wistful smiles while enlightening them as to how desperately you need their custom,' he suggested, tongue in cheek.

Rebel started to laugh. 'I hope you're not insinuating I should trade on my sex in my attempts to gain business, Mr Erskine,' she reproved in well feigned shock.

'Perish the thought, Miss Hayward,' he protested, all innocence. 'Although it does seem something of a waste to have two different sexes if we can't take advantage of it occasionally, don't you think?'

'Quite possibly,' she allowed with another laugh. 'Except that in this instance I think I'd prefer to keep it on a business footing, thanks all the same. I've no wish to be accused of making eyes at someone's husband, and especially when it's usually the wives who do the purchasing.'

'Ah, well, I was only trying to help,' he shrugged impenitently. 'But now, I guess I'd better be moving. Jocelyn will no doubt have finished the mail and be waiting impatiently for me to sign for it. I'll see you tomorrow night, okay?'

'Okay,' she repeated lightly. 'Thank you for calling in, and—and for the advice regarding Van.'

His head dipped slightly in acknowledgment. 'Don't mention it. I just hope everything turns out right for you.'

No more than she did, that was for certain, Rebel sighed to herself as he pushed out through the screen door and she turned for the passage. But perhaps it would all turn out for the best if Van could make a success of the repair shop he was interested in, she tried to cheer herself. And if he couldn't? an insidious thought intruded. She shrugged and refused to think that far ahead. Didn't she already have enough to worry about?

Back in the kitchen she discovered that although her brother had a fully stocked freezer, there were no fresh vegetables to be found—thereby relieving her of the need to prepare any. So she merely took some steak out to give it time to defrost, left the frozen vegetables where they were for the time being, and then made her way back to the store in the hope of locating a tin of potatoes. Eventually she managed to find some on the top shelf, gave a horrified gasp at the price marked thereon, and carried a tin back to the kitchen.

After that it became just a matter of waiting for Van to return, and in order to fill in time she wandered back to the store once more to search for any paperwork she could find relating to the purchasing and pricing of supplies. Apart from the fact that she would shortly need to know such information, the price of those potatoes had come as such a shock that she was extremely interested to discover as soon as possible what prices the store itself paid for its goods.

The papers weren't too difficult to uncover—she came across a whole drawerful of them beneath the till—but sorting them out so she could make sense of them was nowhere near as easy, and in the end she had to spread them over the counter before she could even begin to make headway. She was still puzzling over one account when the creak of the screen door cut into her concentration and had her lifting her head enquiringly.

It wasn't a late customer, however, but Van, who stood facing her with an idiotically pleased look on his face and a bottle of champagne held aloft like a trophy in one hand.

'I've brought us something to celebrate with,' he grinned as he walked towards the counter and gave the bottle a shake. 'I'm sorry I was so long, but I'm not late, am I?'

It wasn't really so much a question as a rather proud statement of fact, for when Rebel checked with her watch it was to find him speaking the truth. It was only six-forty, and he wasn't late!

'No, you're not late,' she confirmed with a rueful half laugh. 'Although I suspect you've done most of your celebrating already.' At this stage she thought it wisest not to mention that Murray had previously brought her that news.

'Four, that's all, I swear!' He held up the appropriate number of fingers as if to make it official. 'I said things were going to be different from now on, and I meant it, Reb!'

'I'm glad,' she smiled warmly, and was thankful too that she had heeded Murray's warning to hear what he had to say first. Gathering up the papers from the counter, she nodded towards the passage and suggested cheerfully, 'If you'd like to put that bottle back on ice for a while I'll get dinner ready. I didn't want to start it until I knew what time you'd be back, but it won't take very long.'

'That's all right, whenever you're ready.' As he came around the counter Van put up a hand to his neatly trimmed hair. 'What do you think of it?' he questioned wryly.

'A great improvement, now you look like the brother I used to know,' she grinned. About to leave the shop, she glanced quickly over her shoulder. 'Should we close the doors?' she queried.

'May as well, I suppose,' he shrugged, and handed her the bottle of champagne before heading back towards them. 'I used to leave them open till about eight most nights when the business was doing okay, but I doubt if anyone will be in tonight.'

Rebel watched as he pulled the doors shut and slid the bolt across, her attention on his last words rather than his actions. 'Did it used to be a flourishing concern, Van?' she asked once he had rejoined her.

He retrieved the champagne and together they made for the kitchen. 'Well, I don't know that I would have called it flourishing exactly, but it certainly had a steady flow of cash coming in,' he replied.

'Judging by the prices marked on some of those tins, a very high cash flow, I would have thought,' drily.

One shoulder was raised unconcernedly. 'I had to get some money somehow when trade started to fall off.'

'So you just kept putting up your prices?'

'What else could I have done?'

Tempted to tell him, Rebel just caught hold of herself in time. That was all in the past now and it would be best if she continued to leave it there. She decided against replying to his question and voiced an enquiry of her own instead.

'Would you mind if I made up a new price list, then? I'm sure some of them are way too high as they are.'

'Whatever you consider best,' he allowed equably as he deposited the wine in the fridge while she put the water on to boil for the vegetables and began heating the grill.

'Don't forget, though, that we're supposed to support ourselves on those proceeds, and as you saw for yourself today, we haven't really been inundated with business.'

That was the truth, and a worrying one, Rebel owned ruefully, and it was only the thought that the store *had* been a viable proposition—and not so very long ago—that gave her any real cause for optimism.

'Mmm, but I'm hoping a smaller profit more often will be of greater value in the long term than a larger profit once every blue moon. That's the policy the chain stores use and it doesn't appear to have done them any harm,' she relayed confidently. She didn't add that it also seemed to have been the successful policy for the Pitereeka store until he had taken over. That was another of those things she considered better left unsaid.

'Well, I'll just wish you the best of luck and steer well clear of it,' Van half laughed. 'Having been such a failure myself, I guess I'm hardly in a position to offer advice. Oh, except for one thing.' He raised a cautioning hand, his expression wry with remembrance. 'Don't waste your time ordering anything chocolate-coated during the summer months. That's one lesson I did learn!'

'The heat spoils it?' she surmised.

'The heat reduces it to a molten ooze ... and that's before it even gets here!'

'I'll keep it in mind,' she vowed with an understanding grin. It was a point worth knowing. With the steaks sizzling on the grill and the vegetables added to the boiling water it reminded Rebel of a question she wanted to ask. 'By the way, I couldn't find any fresh vegetables earlier. Do you usually only eat frozen or tinned out here?'

'Mostly you do if you don't grow your own. Sometimes we get some sent out from Deep Wells but, once again, they're usually pretty unappetising by the time they arrive. Although there's a sack of potatoes in the storeroom down by the shed,' he advised as he watched her empty the contents of her precious can of the commodity into a saucepan.

'Now he tells me!' She wrinkled her nose at him in mock

disgust. 'But they wouldn't last long in the heat either, would they?'

'Oh, they don't do too badly in the storeroom. It's built of double stone and that helps to keep the temperature down.'

'For anything else one has to become a market gardener, though?'

Van didn't say anything, just grinned—meaningfully—and had her pulling just as eloquent a face in return.

'I don't care for gardening much, how about you?' she queried hopefully.

'Sorry.' He shook his head and chuckled, then relented and offered, 'But I'll tell you what. I'll turn over the ground and plant whatever you want put in, if you'll take care of them from then on.'

It sounded reasonable and it was certainly better than doing it all herself. 'You're on!' she accepted his offer before he had a chance to retract it. 'Where do I get the seeds from?'

His telling grin returned as he pointed down the hallway. 'This is a *general* store, remember.'

Rebel laughed at her own lack of thought. 'I keep forgetting. I can see I'll have to go through that shop with a fine tooth comb to discover just what we do sell, otherwise I'm likely to tell someone we don't stock what they're after when we do all the time.'

'You're really looking forward to getting stuck into that shop, aren't you?' His glance was affectionate as he studied her delightfully animated features.

'Yes,' she began slowly. Then, with more vigour, 'Yes, I am. Mind you, I'm not quite sure why, because I really didn't enjoy the years I spent in Uncle Roger's shop, but there's just something about this one that appeals to me. Maybe because it's yours.'

'Not any more it isn't,' Van laughingly but emphatically renounced any responsibility for it. 'I willingly accept ... with thanks!'

*

The next morning Rebel was awake bright and early. Not because she had had a restless night—actually, she had slept a good deal more soundly than she had anticipated—but because, as Van had presupposed the previous evening, she was eager to start cleaning and reorganising the store as her first moves towards its return to a paying enterprise.

She missed the laughing calls of the kookaburras which had often heralded the morning from the park behind her aunt's house, but deduced she was too far inland for their chortling presence. Here, she was far more likely to encounter the screech of sulphur-crested cockatoos or crimson-breasted galahs.

From her bedroom window she could see across one corner of their backyard to the saltbush and bluebush flats beyond which stretched endlessly over the landscape towards a bordering line of purple-smudged hills. It was such a different view from that which she was used to that she continued to stare at it, interestedly and wonderingly, until she remembered the reason for her being out of bed so early, whereupon she gathered up her clothes and set off for the shower.

When she emerged, wearing denim shorts and a loose-fitting muslin blouse, it was to find Van already in the kitchen. Stifling a yawn, he motioned towards a teapot sitting on the table before heading for the bathroom in turn.

'I've made the tea,' he told her sleepily.

'Thank you,' she called after him as he disappeared down the hall. 'What would you like for breakfast?' Sausages and eggs?' She had left some in the fridge to thaw overnight.

He said something in reply which she thought may have been, 'Lovely,' but as it was too indistinct for her to be certain, Rebel shrugged and decided to trust to luck. If he didn't want the sausages they could always cut them up for their sandwiches at lunch time. On his return he soon put paid to that idea, however, by consuming every last particle she placed on his plate.

'That was very nice, thanks, Reb,' he complimented appreciatively as he moved his plate away and brought his teacup closer. 'I haven't had a breakfast like that since ... well, not for months, anyway.'

'Then you should be ashamed of yourself. You obviously had the food here,' she retorted, but with very little sting in her tone. 'It's no wonder I kept thinking you weren't well when I first saw you yesterday.'

'Mmm, yes, if I remember correctly I—er—did have a rather heavy night on Wednesday,' he confessed ruefully, apologetically, then immediately glossed over it by saying, 'But talking of yesterday, I don't think I mentioned that there's a do on this evening over at the hall, did I?'

'No, but Murray did.'

'Oh, that's good.' For some inexplicable reason Van sounded relieved. 'I'm glad it wasn't left to me to tell you that you'd have to give up some of your time in the store today.'

'Come again?' Rebel sought further clarification blankly.

'You know, the cooking.'

'No, I don't know.' She shook her head confusedly. 'What cooking?'

'You mean, he didn't tell you it was a "Ladies Please Provide"?'

'Whatever that may be! No, he didn't—tell—me ...' Her denial tailed off slowly as what he was trying to say suddenly penetrated, and her expression turned to one of utter dismay and disappointment. 'Oh, no, not today! Not when I've so many other things I want to do. It's one of those where the women each provide a couple of plates or so of food, isn't it?' she sighed.

He nodded sympathetically. 'I gather he didn't tell you.'

'You gather right,' she grimaced drily. 'And so it would now be very much appreciated if *you* wouldn't mind explaining just what sort of food I'm expected to provide.'

'Oh, hell, you'd probably have a better idea of that than I would, Reb. It's just sort of ... party food,' he advised helplessly. 'Whatever's easiest for you to make should do, I guess.'

'Sausage rolls, caramel tarts, meringues?'

'Just the thing,' he granted swiftly. So swiftly, in fact, that if she had suggested snails, toads, and lizards, she doubted if he would have had time to change his answer.

'Okay,' she sighed again, fatalistically this time. 'If it's got to be done I suppose I may as well get on with it as soon as possible. The store will just have to wait for a couple of hours longer, I guess.'

'By which time I'll have it all nicely cleaned out for you.'

'Would you?' she smiled at him gratefully.

'As if you need to ask! Of course I will! Don't forget, it's to my advantage too to have the store rearranged as quickly as we can.'

Her blue eyes came alight with a wry gleam. 'So you can wash your hands of it completely and begin organising your own business?' she presumed.

'That's the general idea.' His agreement was laughingly given.

And if the amount of work he had managed to get through during the time she had been confined to the kitchen was to be taken as a guide, then he was very keen indeed to put his ideas for a repair shop into practice, Rebel decided when she was finally able to join him in the store later that morning.

'I wouldn't have believed you could accomplish so much in just a couple of hours!' she marvelled as she took note of all the glossy paintwork which was now visible, where before there had only been accumulated coatings of dust and grime. 'You must have been going flat out the whole time to have managed to have washed the windows and the floor, as well as all those shelves.'

Van accepted her praise with a ready grin, gave a last wipe to the long counter, and dropped the cloth he had been using into a water-filled bucket close by. With his hands resting on his hips he surveyed the finished effect judiciously.

'Yes, well, once I'd cleaned out a corner so I had somewhere to stack everything, there wasn't much to it really. I didn't bother about putting them back again because I thought you'd rather do that so you'd know where everything is.' He slanted her a questioning look. 'How did it go your end?'

'Oh, not too bad. At least everything looks presentable. I had a spot of bother with the sausage rolls because I hurried them a little.' A smile tilted the corners of her mobile mouth. 'I'll have to try one before we leave just to make sure they did cook all the way through. I wouldn't like to trust to luck and then have someone else discover they're still half raw.'

'No need to wait, I'll test them for you right now, if you like,' Van promptly volunteered with a boyish grin.

'Don't you dare! I can remember you offering to taste some butterfly cakes Mum had made for a birthday of mine years ago . . . and you ate the lot!'

'Good grief, fancy you still remembering that,' he laughed. 'You could only have been six or seven at the time.'

'Old enough for it to have made a lasting impression, though . . . luckily!' she retorted in bantering tones.

'Huh!' He pretended to take affront. 'Well, isn't that lovely? I offer to put my stomach in jeopardy in an effort to save you some embarrassment, and . . .'

'Out!' She pointed dramatically towards the bead curtain. 'Put your stomach in jeopardy indeed! There'll be other sections of your anatomy in worse danger if you stay around here much longer, I can assure you!'

He headed cheerfully for the doorway without waiting for another bidding. 'Oh, yes, that's the way. Now I've done all the hard work just kick me out,' he complained in mock reproach.

'Well, if you're that eager to stay, you could always . . .'

'No, I'll go,' he interrupted swiftly. 'I don't need to be told twice that I'm not wanted.'

Rebel grinned as he disappeared along the passage. She didn't need to be told twice that he would rather be elsewhere either! He was as anxious to surrender all responsibility for the store as she was to assume it.

A few minutes later, after disposing of the buckets, mops, and cloths Van had used, and armed with the new price list she had made out the previous evening, she began erasing the old amounts marked on the various tins and packets and replacing most of them was less exorbitant ones as she systematically returned them to the shelves. It was a slow process and although she had been at it for some time the pile of goods on the floor didn't appear to have decreased greatly when the gauze door opened and her first customer walked in, a young woman with soft brown eyes and a pleasant smile.

'Good morning, I'm Denise Aldridge,' she introduced herself immediately. 'I guess you must be Van's sister, right?'

'Yes, I'm Rebel,' came the wry, half laughing return. By now, probably everyone in town would know she had arrived. 'How do you do?'

'Not so good at the moment, I'm sorry to say,' the other girl revealed with a grimace. 'I was part way through making a fruit cake for the party tonight when I found I was out of glacé cherries, so I thought I'd trot down here and see if you perhaps had any.'

'I know Van has kept them at some time because I saw them listed on one of his orders last night,' Rebel supplied pensively, then motioned towards the jumbled mounds of goods. 'Unfortunately, though, we're in rather a mess today because Van's taken everything off the shelves so I can reorganise them. If you don't mind waiting a minute I'll sift through them and see if I can find some for you.'

'I'll give you a hand,' offered Denise helpfully. 'It looks as if you might need it with that load.'

'You could be right,' Rebel conceded with a rueful smile. 'While it was on the shelves it didn't look terribly much, but altogether like this . . . well, that's something else again.'

Both girls crouched down beside the merchandise and began moving articles aside in their search, their conversation continuing desultorily as they did so.

'You live here in town, I gather?' Rebel spoke first.

'Mmm, the house on the other side of the post office. Malcolm—my husband—works as a stockman for the Seftons on Trinity Station.'

'I always thought stockmen lived on the properties where they worked,' Rebel commented in some surprise.

Denise shook her head and explained, 'Most of the single men do, but not always the married ones. It depends on the size of the property—some of them don't have much married accommodation—and whether there's a town handy.'

'So all the people who live in town are employed by the surrounding properties, are they?'

'More or less,' came the agreement, followed by a qualifying, 'Though some only indirectly. Like the Lamberts, they're fencing contractors. And Burt Deakin and Chris Hanson, they're shearers. Then, of course, there's old Daisy and Dudley Ruddock.'

'Oh, and what do they do?' queried Rebel interestedly.

'They're a retired couple who arrived out of the blue about a year ago to do some prospecting, and they're determined they're going to make a big find, if it's the last thing they do.'

'A big find of what?'

'Anything and everything, I think!' Denise laughed. 'But you'll see them driving off at the same time each morning —and just where they go no one is absolutely certain—then back they come each afternoon looking very pleased with themselves, but with hardly a thing to show for their day's efforts.'

'Maybe they're keeping it a secret.'

This idea was discounted quickly. 'No, that would be a physical impossibility. Even if it's only a strangely shaped rock Daisy can't wait to show everyone.'

'Oh, well, as long as they're happy doing what they're doing,' murmured Rebel vaguely as she tried to push an unopened carton of tinned fruit to one side in order to look behind it. She wasn't able to move it far, just enough to show the corner of a familiar-looking packet and have her exclaiming, 'I think I see some!' as she tugged all the harder at the heavy box.

'Can I be of any assistance?'

Two heads swung round in unison at the unexpected sound of a male voice behind them and although Rebel didn't know the newcomer, Denise obviously did.

'Yes, thanks, Steve,' she accepted his offer speedily. 'Move this out of the way, will you, please?'

The young man in the faded shirt and dusty jeans raised a finger to his equally dusty hat and grinned obligingly as he stepped forward and hefted the case effortlessly into his arms.

'Where to?' he queried goodnaturedly.

'Er—the counter, I think, please,' Rebel responded with a grateful smile. 'It will save me having to carry all those tins so far when I come to empty it.'

No sooner said than accomplished, Denise swooped gleefully on to the packet which had created the need for its removal. 'You were right, it was them, Rebel! How much do I owe you?'

A hasty consultation with her list and Rebel lowered the price by about twenty cents from that which was noted on the package.

'But it says more than that on here,' Denise puzzled as she turned the packet over in her hand.

'Yes, well, it's on special this week,' Rebel said the first thing that came into her head. She didn't want it made too obvious just how much profit Van had been making out of everyone! And in an attempt to make it sound more creditable, she explained, 'I made out a list last night from some of Van's orders with the idea that if he still had those items in stock I'd reduce all the prices for next week.'

'In that case, I'll take both the packets you've got left,' said the other girl, and bent to retrieve the remaining one as well. 'I'm sure to want more of them before Christmas is over.' While Rebel counted out her required change she suddenly apologised, 'Oh, look, I'm sorry, I don't suppose you two know each other, do you? Steve Maitland—Rebel Hayward,' she rectified the omission with a smile.

Rebel returned the young man's ensuing greeting readily. She estimated him to be about her own age and he had an open relaxed manner which she found very easy to respond to.

Their acknowledgments concluded, Denise sent him a measuring glance. 'How come you're in town at this time of day, Steve?' she probed interestedly, and not a little teasingly. 'Come to check out our newest visitor for yourself, hmm?'

If she had thought to see him discomfited then she was doomed to disappointment, because his self-possession didn't waver in the slightest. 'As much as the idea appealed, I did at least wait until I had a reasonably legitimate excuse,' he admitted in a lazy drawl, smiling.

'*Reasonably* legitimate?' Denise wasn't above pursuing, eyeing him banteringly.

'I was checking the windmill in one of the paddocks a few miles out of town when I leant over and lost my smokes out of my shirt pocket into the turkey's nest. Naturally I had to come in to replace them,' he claimed without so much as a blink.

'Oh, naturally!' grinned Denise with a smothered gurgle.

Rebel looked from one to the other. 'Turkey's nest?' she quizzed in a perplexed tone.

It was left to Steve to elucidate. 'That's the reservoir the windmill pumps water into from a bore.'

'Now I understand,' she nodded ruefully. Then, recalling his reason for being there, she asked, 'Which brand of cigarettes were you after?'

When he told her she promptly exchanged a laughing look with the older girl. 'You didn't happen to see them in your search for the cherries, did you, Denise?'

'I don't know about that particular make, but I did see some ...' she paused momentarily, closing her eyes as she tried to remember. 'Oh, yes, I think they were somewhere underneath the detergent and the fly spray.'

Rebel started for the corner once more. 'Well, that at least gives me something to go on.'

'And as much as I'd like to stay and help, I guess I'd better be going, otherwise I'll never have anything ready for tonight,' Denise advised as she headed in the opposite direction. 'I'll see you both later.'

'Sure thing.'

'See you, Denise, and thanks for the help.'

The two separate replies followed her through the doorway and then Steve sank down on to his haunches next to Rebel, watching for a minute or so as she rummaged through the increasingly untidy heap.

'You know, you'll only need to have a couple more customers and you're not going to be able to find anything in there,' he commented with undeniable logic.

'I know,' she sighed, and stopped her searching for a moment. 'But until I have a chance to get them all back on the shelves there's not much I can do about it.'

'Then you'll just have to get them back there quicker. Come on, I'll give you a hand.' He rose agilely upright, then helped her to her feet too. 'It shouldn't take long with two of us. Besides, some of those cartons are too heavy for you to be lifting, anyway.'

She might not have been able to dispute his last statement, but she did have something to say about the other. 'Steve, I very much appreciate your offer, but I can't just take you away from your own work like that,' she protested, round-eyed. 'Whatever would your boss say?'

He shrugged and grinned. 'He'd have to find out first.'

Rebel couldn't suppress a smile at such frankness, but she still shook her head vehemently. 'No, it's very nice of you, but I can't accept. Not only would it be unfair for you to take the risk while I receive the benefit, but I'd feel as guilty as hell the whole time you were here.' She swept a stray lock of hair back over her shoulder and pointed out excusingly, 'In any case, if I really get stuck I can always call on Van. He only left me with it today because he knew I was wanting to tackle it on my own.'

'Okay, I'll just lend a hand till you come across the cigar-ettes,' he compromised, and evidently convinced it was too much for her to do alone. 'How's that?'

'All right, that I'll accept,' she gave in with a laugh. This way she wouldn't be keeping him away from his work any longer than she would have done by her haphazard search-ing, and she *could* do with some help with a few of the larger items.

As Steve had so rightly predicted, the shelves rapidly began to fill with two of them working at it, and as he handed the articles across she placed them in position. She wasn't bothering to alter the prices this time, though. That could be done at a later date, she decided, once she had everything where she wanted it.

It did seem to be taking a very long time for him to unearth the cigarettes, however, and during a rare moment when she had caught up to him she shot a frowning glance towards the decidedly smaller mounds.

'Steve!' she promptly exclaimed in a mixture of dismay and wry exasperation. 'You're not supposed to be opening the new boxes, you're supposed to be looking for the cigarettes! Denise said they were beneath the detergent and the fly spray and we've done those. Haven't you found them yet?'

'Wrong brands,' he smiled up at her complacently.

Uncertain whether to believe him or not, Rebel looked past him again. 'Oh, they are not!' she retorted as a dis-tinctive wrapper captured her attention and, coming down from the small step-ladder she had been using, she hur-ried around the counter to pounce on a rectangular carton which she immediately proceeded to split open. 'These are the ones you were after, aren't they?' she challenged drily.

'So they are.' His blue eyes laughed into hers.

Trying to look annoyed, she soon realised she just wasn't going to make it, and smiled back. 'Just the one packet?'

He nodded and withdrew a ten-dollar note from his hip pocket in payment.

A quick look in the till was sufficient to convince her she

didn't have enough change, and with an excusing, 'Sorry, I'll have to get some more notes from inside,' she set off down the hall.

When she returned it was to find him calmly opening a box of tinned meat and stacking the contents neatly on the shelves. Taking a deep breath, she thrust the money she carried into his hand and eyed him in something close to despair.

'Steven Maitland ... *go home*!' she wailed helplessly. 'As much as I appreciate your help, you've been here for ... oh, my God!' she gasped on checking with her watch, 'nearly two hours! Please go back to work.' Her eyes sought his beseechingly.

'As soon as we've finished these,' he agreed, returning her gaze with an assuring smile. 'They're the last of the heavy ones.'

'You promise?' It seemed the best she was going to get.

'So help me!' he averred positively.

'It had better be,' she muttered direfully, and began climbing the step-ladder. Half a dozen tins later she halted and sent him as extremely graphic smile. 'You know, if your boss ever finds out about this, he's going to tear strips off both our hides!'

'You're so right!' declared a deeply disturbing voice from the doorway, and had two suddenly watchful faces simultaneously swinging in that direction.

CHAPTER SIX

REBEL swallowed convulsively as she took in Chayne Cavanagh's unexpected and, for her, totally imbalancing presence. That evocative aura of vibrant maleness which seemed such an integral part of his personality was affecting her just as disconcertingly as it had at their initial meeting, she noted with a dismal sigh. And that was without him even turning those alert green-hued eyes of his her way, because right at the moment all his concentration was directed towards the young man standing at the foot of the step-ladder.

'You finished your work for the day, Steve?' The question was clipped out tautly. A shade sarcastically too, in Rebel's mind.

'No, not yet, boss.'

The answer had Rebel's eyes widening in alarm. It was Chayne who was Steve's employer? Until that moment she had been too occupied in attempting to control the calamitous feelings his appearance had aroused to analyse his opening statement. She had merely taken it to be a sardonic —but uninvolved agreement with her last remark. Now that she knew differently she clambered swiftly down from her perch, intent on doing what she could to relieve the pressure on her obliging helper.

'Look, I'm sorry, but it really wasn't Steve's fault. He only . . .'

'Wait your turn, honey! I'm coming to you!' Chayne's voice sliced through her explanation like a knife. Then, turning his back on her, he indicated with his head for the younger man to follow him outside.

Steve's almost imperceptible wink as he passed her did nothing to calm Rebel's flaring indignation at having been so summarily rebuffed, however, although she could have wished for some of the young man's self-possession. She couldn't doubt that his coming interview with his employer was likely to be anything but pleasant, and yet he appeared completely unperturbed by the thought of it.

Inside, their voices only reached her as an indistinct murmur, and for only an ominously short time, which was followered by a brief period of silence before the sound of a motorbike being kicked into life took over. Guessing her condemnation was to be next on the agenda, Rebel swiveller around hastily and rushed back up the three steps of the ladder to busy herself altering prices. At least from up there she would have the advantage of him having to look up to her!

From the corner of her eye she saw Steve disappear past the window on the bike and felt an uncomfortable trickle of apprehension slither down her spine as determined footsteps paced ever closer towards the counter. But she refused to acknowledge having heard them by so much as the slightest turning of her head.

'I'd like a word with you, Miss Hayward! If it's not too much trouble, that is!' he grated finally in an infuriated tone heavily spiked with sarcasm when it became apparent she had no intention of facing him.

'Well, I am rather busy at the moment, Mr Cavanagh.' She put one tin back and prepared to pick up another.

'Then it will my pleasure to make it short ... and *explicit*!'

Inexorable fingers bit deeply into the slender curves of her waist and within seconds she had been swung uncermoniously off her feet and tossed over a heavily muscled leg as Chayne settled himself on the top step of the ladder. It all happened so rapidly that, apart from her first startled gasp of shock, Rebel had no time to struggle or protest until the forerunner of a series of stinging slaps from the palm of an unbelievably hard hand landed on the seat of her shorts. Then she made up for lost time.

'Oh, how dare you! You barbarian, you *primitive*!' she heaved furiously as she fought against the restraining arm which relentlessly kept her captive. 'Take your hands off me, you brute, and let me *go*!'

His partial compliance with her last enraged command came about suddenly, but only in so far as she was spun back on to her feet. The hands which gripped her shoulders shook her none too gently and had her hair tumbling about her mutinous face in a mass of bright colour.

'Don't you ever dare commandeer any of my staff again! Do you hear?' he blazed.

Unmindful of the angry tears dampening her flushed

cheeks, Rebel was only concerned with breaking free and she wrenched at his arms with ineffectual fingers.

'I hate you!' she lashed back at him fiercely. 'You're nothing but a savage, and a ...'

'*Do you hear?*' He shook her again.

'Yes, I hear!' she flared on a choking breath. 'But don't you ever dare treat me like a child again either, or I'll— I'll ...'

'Tear strips off my hide instead?' One corner of his mouth quirked crookedly.

'Oh, yes, treat it as a joke!' she commended bitterly, dashing the tears from her cheeks with her fingertips. 'No doubt it's very amusing for you to prop up your male ego at the expense of someone weaker than yourself. I notice you didn't attack Steve physically, though! Did you think he might be able to defend himself better than I could?' she gibed.

'No, I simply meted out the punishments I thought most suitable,' he retorted disdainfully.

Rebel's chin angled challengingly higher, her expression one of scornful mockery. 'And conveniently left the corporal chastisement for the person least likely to be able to defend themself!'

'It seemed appropriate.' His accompanying smile was sardonically taunting. 'If you want to behave irresponsibly, expect to be treated the same way.'

'There are other ways of getting messages across, you know!' she fired back instantly, caustically, as her temper soared still higher at his arbitrary attitude. 'Or perhaps you've spent so much of your time incarcerated in those hills you've never learnt how men are supposed to treat members of the opposite sex!'

'Oh, that comes naturally,' he drawled in goading accents as his hands slid from her shoulders to thread through the hair on either side of her face, and he set his lips to hers provokingly.

And for him, it *did* seem to come naturally, Rebel was forced into conceding—though grudgingly—on finding her-

self involuntarily responding to the tempting contact, and
feeling the blood beginning to course restively through her
veins. Her initial move for freedom had been quelled
smoothly, but unhesitatingly, and now she was lashing
herself inwardly for not having the willpower to even try to
continue resisting him. There was a sensuous quality to his
kisses which was relentlessly undermining all her defences
and she knew, notwithstanding her limited experience, that
in Chayne Cavanagh she was dealing with no novice in the
art of making love.

Never had she been kissed so persuasively, nor so
thoroughly, and never had she encountered such a physical
attraction before. It was as if her emotions had run out of
control—or were being manipulated by the man whose
mouth was kindling hitherto unknown sensations within
her—and against such an adept and stirring arousal she was
absolutely helpless.

Only when he saw fit to release her could she regain any
sort of dominance over her capricious feelings and, with
her cheeks burning with embarrassment at the thought of
her barely contested submission, she immediately set out
to protect herself as best she could.

'That wasn't what I was meaning ... as if you didn't
know!' she stormed, albeit raggedly, alluding to his last
remark. 'And for your information, that arrogant piece of
effrontery appealed no more than your previous abominable
treatment!'

'Mmm, I could tell.' His eyes filled with lazy devilry.
'Your resistance was almost overpowering.'

Rebel crimsoned to the roots of her hair. 'Oh, you worm!
As if I—as if you could ever ... oh, why don't you just get
out of here, Chayne!' she hurled at him distractedly. She
had never felt quite so humiliated in all her life! 'You must
have finished all you came to say—and do—by now,
surely!' she couldn't help jeering in conclusion.

'Even if it wasn't, I guess it will just have to suffice for
the present,' Chayne allowed enigmatically, shrugging, and
making for the doorway with lithe strides. With one hand

on the screen door he turned back, his expression anything but indefinable now as he provoked, 'You're obviously in no frame of mind to discuss business.'

Did he mean what she thought he meant? Rebel drew a sharp intake of breath and glared wrathfully at his reparting figure. The heel! He knew how much Mount Cavanagh's custom would mean to the store and yet he had purposely refrained from mentioning it until he was on the point of leaving!

Another fulminating look was directed towards the street as she debated whether she should call him back or not, and then, with a disgruntled sigh, she decided against it. That was probably just what he was wanting, to have her condoning his despicable behaviour by chasing after him, and she flatly refused to give him that much satisfaction, even if it was to the store's detriment. But next time they met it would be a different matter, she promised herself fervently. She would make certain he didn't get a second opportunity to accuse her of not being in the right mood to discuss it!

The sky was a brilliant red, streaked with purple, and the nightly chorus of chirping insects just beginning when Rebel and her brother set out to walk to the hall that evening. It had been a very hot day and the earth was still warm beneath their feet as they paced leisurely towards the brightly lit building. Already the paddock beside it was filled with vehicles of all descriptions and the later arrivals were having to park on either side of the road. A group of laughing children came rushing down the front steps to lose themselves among the stationary vehicles, playing hide and seek, their shrieks and squeals on being tagged bringing a smile to Rebel's lips.

'It didn't occur to me there would be children here as well, although I should have expected it, I suppose. Their parents could hardly leave them at home on their own, could they?' she grinned wryly.

'Not really,' Van laughed with her. 'There'll be more of them here than usual tonight too, what with the older ones being home from boarding school for the summer holidays.'

She took in the size of the hall with a judicious eye. 'Then, at a guess, I'd say it's going to be very crowded.'

'You'd better believe it!'

Almost to the building, Rebel looked up quickly in surprise when two male shapes suddenly appeared, one on either side of them.

'Man, but don't you look different from when we saw you last,' one of them remarked to her brother with a somewhat snide laugh. 'How about an introduction to the miracle worker, huh?'

For a time it seemed as if Van wasn't going to comply. Not that Rebel would have cared. She didn't think she was going to like this pair of heavy-set, bold-eyed young men. But eventually he shrugged and motioned first towards the one who had spoken.

'Morris and Walter Lambert—my sister Rebel,' he divulged brusquely.

'Just call me Walt,' urged the one next to her. She guessed him to be the younger, although not by much, and somewhere in his mid-twenties. His eyes roamed over her insolently and he bent his head conspiratorially close. 'Are you really a rebel like your name says?' he smirked.

There was something faintly suggestive in the way he said it and Rebel quickened her step in a bid to be free of them sooner. 'Only when it comes to rebelling against people I dislike,' she retorted acidly.

'Is that so?' His eyes narrowed suspiciously. 'Then it's just as well we're going to be friends, isn't it? Especially since we hold the mortgage on that store of Van's, and which he's kindly given us leave to call in any time we choose,' he countered pointedly.

Rebel turned to her brother swiftly, a worried question on her lips, but before she could voice it, the elder Lambert was confirming her worst fears.

'That's right,' he grinned cheerfully. 'Ol' Van was so anxious to get his hands on that loan he was willing to agree to anything we suggested!'

'Don't worry, you'll get your money,' Van snapped as he put an arm around Rebel to usher her up the steps and into the hall.

'Oh, that was never in doubt. Our only problem is whether to take it in cash or in kind,' Walter sniggered.

Entering the festively decorated lobby, Rebel cast a dismayed glance sideways. 'Does he mean they'll take the store if they don't get the money soon?' she whispered to her brother.

'I shouldn't pay too much mind to their insinuations, if I were you. I think they've got their hands full at the moment with other ventures. They won't want the store round their necks as well.'

'But you did give them the right to claim it in forfeit at any time?'

'Hell, I don't know! I can't remember what I damn well signed!' He raked a hand irritably through his hair. 'Why don't you just forget about it and enjoy yourself? I told you they won't be doing anything about it.'

'You also told me you didn't think they were expecting you to make any repayments either,' she reminded him a little resentfully. It wasn't her fault they had this threat hanging over them. 'So if they weren't anticipating money, and you reckon they don't want the store, just how were they expecting to be repaid?'

'Oh, with the store, I suppose. But that was before.'

'Before what?'

'I just told you,' he sighed exasperatedly. 'Before they had more important matters to keep them occupied.' He drew a deep breath, then released it slowly, a regretful smile catching at his mouth. 'I'm sorry, Reb, I know I've got no one to blame but myself, but do what I suggested, hmm? Forget it and enjoy yourself. It'll work out okay, you'll see.'

He was trying to be reassuring and she managed a complaisant smile in response, for his sake, but her thoughts weren't nearly so easily pacified. No matter how occupied they might be, she wouldn't put it past the Lamberts to demand immediate payment out of sheer perversity if something, or someone, upset them. Now she was beginning to wish she had chased after Chayne Cavanagh that afternoon—and to blazes with her pride—because the best way to nullify the Lamberts' claims was to repay the loan as soon as possible, but she needed more trade for the store before that could happen.

Her troubled musings were interrupted by introductions to the two men who were collecting the entrance fees, and who turned out to be the two shearers Denise had spoken of earlier. Then they were continuing on into the hall itself, where the first things to attract her attention were the decorations. The cypress pine Christmas tree standing to one side of the stage at the far end with its branches laden down beneath coloured lights, tinsel, and shiny ornaments. The bunches of greenery tied with red ribbons, and the scarlet and black desert peas which adorned the walls, while overhead there were masses of suspended balloons and multicoloured streamers.

A dance was already in progress and between the gaily dressed throng keeping time to a disco beat, Rebel could periodically make out some trestle tables along one side of the room.

'Is that where these go?' she enquired, nodding to the food containers they were both carrying.

Before Van could reply, however, the tin she was clasping was abruptly whisked out of her arms and precariously balanced on top of her brother's load by Walter. He and the older Morris had, apparently, followed them in.

'Van'll get rid of those for you while we're dancing,' he declared confidently as he fastened his fingers firmly about her wrist and took a step forward, tugging her after him.

Indignation and distaste gave Rebel the strength to jerk out of his hold and her eyes sparked fire from within their long lashes. 'If you don't mind, I'd rather take the tins over to the tables myself, thanks very much!' she flared angrily.

'Besides, your first dance is booked with me, isn't it, little one?' From out of the blue Murray's welcome voice sud-

denly sounded next to her and she spun to face him with a
heartfelt sigh of relief and gratitude.

'And even if it wasn't, you keep your hands off my sister,
Walt, or there'll be trouble, believe me!' threatened Van
irately.

Walter was openly scornful. 'Is that supposed to worry
me? That the town drunk's likely to get upset?' He thrust
his face menacingly clear. 'Listen, *mate*, I could take you
apart with ...'

'Okay, Walt, *cool it*! The last thing we need is trouble
over some bird!'

Surprisingly, it was Morris who called a halt to the confrontation and Rebel was thankful to see the younger
Lambert shrug himself back under control, even though he
couldn't forgo a sneered, 'It wouldn't even be a contest!' as
he strode away.

For a time there was silence as they watched the two de-
parting figures and then Rebel made to reclaim her cake tin
from Van.

'No, leave it,' he half smiled, and shook his head, already
starting to move. 'I'll take them across. You go and dance
with Murray.'

'But we hadn't really ...' He was gone before she was
part way through her explanation and she smiled apologetically at the man left with her. 'Sorry, but it looks as if
you're stuck with me. He apparently didn't realise you only
said that about our having arranged the first dance in order
to outmanoeuvre Walter.' She smiled again, gratefully. 'For
which I do thank you.'

Murray brushed her appreciation aside casually. 'You're
welcome. I could see you weren't exactly enamoured with
the idea of dancing with him. However, be that as it may,'
he grinned, 'I can assure you I do not regard it as being
stuck to have such an attractive and alluring female left in
my charge. And so, if you're agreeable, I would be very
pleased to have this dance with you, little one.'

A trifle selfconscious after what she considered to be his
exaggerated compliment, Rebel smiled her acceptance shyly

and followed him on to the floor. Her thoughts returned of
their own accord to the Lamberts almost as soon as she
began moving to the music.

'Van isn't likely to find that man wanting to take up
where he left off later tonight, is he?' she queried worriedly.

'Who, Walt?' He gave a negative shake of his head. 'No,
he might be something of a brawler down at the pub, but
he wouldn't dare start anything like that up here with all
the women and kids around.'

'Thank heavens for that!' At least that was one of her
worries disposed of. 'I've met three of the family so far,
but I can't honestly say I've cared for any of them.'

'Well, if it's any consolation, you're not alone on that
score. I don't think they've endeared themselves much to
anyone in town since they moved here a year or so ago.'

'Oh, they're not really what you would call locals, then?'

'More like itinerant workers,' he explained. 'You know,
they spend some time here, some there, wherever they can
find work.'

'They must have found Pitereeka profitable, then, to have
stayed for so long, and to have been able to lend Van the
money they did,' she speculated pensively.

'Mmm, they did get some good fencing contracts.
They're not bad at their work, I've been told. As to the
other,' he shrugged and didn't quite meet her gaze, 'well,
I expect that was only more or less what he, or some other
poor devil, had already lost to them gambling.'

Rebel was so taken aback that she stopped dancing. 'You
mean it was the Lamberts Van lost it all to in the first
place?' she gasped in disbelief.

His confirmation was closer to a wince than a smile and
she moved her head despairingly.

'Well, wasn't that convenient!' she charged drily. 'I bet
they used to rub their hands in glee every time they saw
him coming.'

'Unfortunately, no one could convince him of that.'

'In other words, there's none so blind as those who don't
want to see.'

His smile was sympathetic. 'I'm afraid so.'

'Oh, well, I guess there's nothing that can be done about it now.' She pulled a rueful face and picked up the rhythm of the band again. 'I'm glad I arrived before he managed to fritter away everything he'd worked for, though.'

Presently, as the music changed to a slower beat and Murray took her in his arms, Rebel caught sight of a strikingly dressed blonde with familiar features a short distance away and her eyes widened in astonishment.

'I didn't expect to see Karina Loudon here tonight!' she exclaimed. 'I thought she said she had no use for Pitereeka.'

Murray's lips twisted sardonically. 'Ah, but tonight there's a very good reason for her presence.'

'The Christmas party?' She wouldn't have thought it would rate that highly among the other girl's social engagements.

'Don't be slow, little one,' he chided mockingly. 'I'm sure you got the message very clearly in Deep Wells as to just what the attraction was for Karina out this way.'

'Oh, you mean ...' She started to smile, then stopped and gulped, '*Chayne's* here too?' That was something else she hadn't expected!

'Of course he is. All the Cavanaghs are,' he grinned at her startled expression. 'Why wouldn't they be? I suppose you'd say this is the nearest thing they've got to a home town.'

'I guess so. I just didn't think,' she offered weakly, her mind racing.

Although she wanted to see Chayne with regard to the store, she wasn't at all sure she was ready to meet him for a second time that day. The events of the afternoon were still very much to the forefront of her thoughts and, not the least disquieting of which was the fact that, each time her temper flared at the idea of him having the temerity to turn her over his knee, it was immediately cancelled by an even stronger urge to concentrate on the tantalising few minutes which had followed. With a start she realised she was inadvertently doing the same again right now, and she shut the disturbing pictures from her mind resolutely as she took a hasty look over her shoulder to where she had last seen Karina.

'That wasn't him dancing with her,' she relayed in as natural and as indifferent a tone as possible.

'No?' The corners of Murray's mouth turned down cynically. 'Well, maybe he's managed to give her the slip for the time being.'

'He's not interested in *her*?' Heaven only knew why that thought should have occasioned such a feeling of cheerfulness.

One shoulder was hunched in a gesture of ignorance. 'As to that, I wouldn't be knowing,' he unwittingly sent her hopes crashing. 'Chayne keeps his private life exactly that —*private*—and in all the time I've known him he hasn't yet let me know how he feels about any of the women he's been seen with. And take my word for it, there's been some!'

A declaration she could well believe! That rugged virility of Chayne's would attract women like a flame did moths and, probably, with just as disastrous consequences, she surmised in a sudden inexplicable fit of depression.

'No, that was just my own personal aversion showing when I said he may have given her the slip,' Murray continued with a wry half laugh. 'Karina and I aren't really what you would call buddy-buddy. We speak when it can't be avoided, but for preference we'd rather give each other a wide berth.'

Rebel's lips pursed meditatively. 'Now that I come to think of it, you weren't particularly talkative that evening in Deep Wells, nor did you spend much time at the table. Was she the reason?'

'In part.'

She peered at him closely, wondering at the dryness in his tone, and then grinned broadly. 'Oh, yes, if I remember correctly, you also had someone else on your mind that night, didn't you?' A cursory look round the room, although she wasn't sure for whom, and she was querying interestedly, 'Is she here tonight?'

He gave a rueful laugh, shaking his head. 'No, she's working tonight. She's a nurse at the Deep Wells hospital and she started a week's night duty yesterday. You'll meet her at young Wendy Metcalfe's wedding next Saturday, though.'

All thoughts of asking him his girl-friend's name now fled as amazed questions on her own behalf began pouring forth. 'A wedding? On Saturday? How can I go to someone's wedding when I've never even met them? Who is Wendy Metcalfe, anyway? Does she live here in town?'

'Hold it!' He sued for a respite in an amused voice, one hand raised high as if for protection. 'Not so fast, or I'll never be able to remember them all. Firstly, Wendy is the youngest daughter of Chayne's overseer. No doubt you'll get to meet her some time this evening but, just for the record, that's her and Greg, the chap she's marrying, over there.' He surreptitiously pointed out two figures standing about halfway down the hall. 'The seated couple they're talking to are her parents, Dan and Thelma.'

As the music ceased and they began making their way from the middle of the floor, a covert glance was cast in the direction he had indicated and Rebel studied the foursome quickly. The younger pair stood close together, their arms draped loosely about each other's waists, the girl a blue-eyed brunette in her late teens, her fiancé a solidly built blond in his early twenties. The girl's parents, she found, were a contented-looking couple who, if their happy expressions were anything to judge by, were completely in accord with their daughter's choice of a husband.

'Right!' She returned her attention to Murray with a grin. 'That settles who she is and where she lives. I presume she does live on the property with her parents?' Confirmed by a nod, she continued, 'Now, perhaps, you'd better just explain why I'm expected to be going to her wedding.'

'Mainly, because just about everyone from town is going,

but especially because Van used to work on the station and consequently knows the whole family quite well. He's going,' he assured her knowledgeably.

'He hasn't mentioned anything about it to me!'

'Probably because your unexpected arrival has pushed it to the back of his mind.'

It was feasible. 'Where's the wedding taking place?' she enquired next, frowningly. 'I haven't noticed a church anywhere in town.'

'Actually, you're standing in it,' he advised drily. 'The hall also doubles as the church when the minister, priest, preacher, make their rounds. However, the wedding's to be held at Mount Cavanagh. In God's own church, you might say.'

'Meaning?'

'Outdoors.' His enlightenment came with a smile. 'With the warm earth as the floor, the green hills as walls, and a cloudless blue sky for a roof.'

'Well, well, and to think I never suspected you of having such a romantic turn of mind,' she couldn't pass up the opportunity to tease, even though she thoroughly approved of the idea. 'Are there any other similar secrets hidden beneath that stalwart exterior, I wonder?'

'Some very *un*romantic ones right at present, if you must know,' he retorted, and made a mock-threatening grab for her.

Laughing, she took a hurried step backwards and promptly cannoned into someone behind her. 'Oh, I'm sorry,' she looked up quickly to apologise as a pair of strong, steadying hands came to rest on the silken skin of her bare shoulders.

But on discovering just whose hands retained their hold on her, and on encountering alert hazel-green eyes surveying her upturned face so disturbingly, her demeanour underwent a dramatic change as undeniable attraction swamped her.

'I'm not talking to you, Chayne!' she burst out defensively, resentfully, completely forgetting for the moment that that was exactly what she had resolved to do the next time they met.

'I think you're about to cop what I got yesterday afternoon,' inserted a smiling Murray for his friend's benefit. He was obviously under the impression that this was the first time Rebel had seen the other man since the previous Tuesday. 'We're in the gun for not having told her the truth about Van.'

'Oh?' Chayne's well defined mouth quirked humorously as he fixed Rebel with a gleaming gaze. 'That's why I'm getting the cold shoulder, is it?'

At least two of those present knew that wasn't so, but she was determined she wasn't going to be the one to inform the third person of that fact, and she valiantly returned his look with eyes which glittered just as tauntingly.

'Didn't you expect to be?' she quipped facetiously.

'Murray seems to have been forgiven.'

It was too good an opening to miss, regardless of what ensued. 'And is that what you're asking for ... forgiveness?'

'I know what *you're* asking for!' he laughed, and had her bones turning to liquid at the beguiling sound of it. A hand snaked out to capture her wrist and his eyes challenged hers discomposingly. 'Come and dance with me, and we'll see if we can't work out a compromise.'

'I—I was going to look for Van,' she parried, nervous now as a kind of fluttering panic beset her. It was no use expecting Murray to help, he was too busy chuckling at what was happening.

'You can do that afterwards. He's not going anywhere.'

Inexorably she was drawn towards the dance floor as the band struck up again, and her heart sank on hearing the slow number they had chosen to play. It might at least have been an up-tempo tune, she despaired.

Chayne swung her smoothly into his arms, his head lowering to within inches of hers. 'Well?' he drawled mockingly.

'I told you, I'm not talking to you,' she flouted smugly,

figuring silence was her best means of defence and protection.

'Okay, no compromise,' he shrugged with apparent indifference. Except that his accompanying actions weren't disinterested, they were wholly disturbing from Rebel's standpoint as the hand at her back moulded her even closer to his muscled length, and instead of being lifted his head was lowered still further, his lips proceeding to send spine-tingling tremors throughout her nervous system as they deliberately sought out the ultra-sensitive areas down the side of her neck.

'Chayne!' she protested agitatedly, and unsuccessfully trying to twist free of the shattering contact. It had never entered her mind that this might be his method of retaliation for her earlier attempt to provoke, and her capitulation came swiftly, desperately, before he could devastate her emotions any further. 'All right, all right, you win! What sort of compromise did you have in mind?'

To her relief he raised his head at that, although the look in his eyes when they caught and held hers was almost as demolishing as the touch of his mouth had been.

'Preferably one which gives me the edge,' he revealed drily. 'I have a feeling I'm going to need it where you're concerned, honey.'

She made a disgruntled moue. 'I don't see why. You've had everything your own way so far.'

'Mmm, but don't worry, I'm sure your turn's coming.'

'I seem to recall you saying something similar to that this afternoon ... just before you laid hands on me in a most ungentlemanly fashion,' she accused reproachfully.

His teeth gleamed whitely in a wry smile and had her swallowing convulsively. 'Is that a hint for an apology?'

'Am I likely to get one?' she countered with sardonic overtones.

'That depends.' He hunched one shoulder impassively. 'Are *you* intending to offer one?'

'Me!' she was startled into exclaiming. 'I was the one on the receiving end, remember?'

'But not without reason, if you care to cast your mind a little further back, hmm?'

'Oh, you mean Steve! But I tried to apologise for that!' The recollection came to her suddenly. 'That was when you told me to wait my turn!'

'You're lucky that's all I said,' he retorted succinctly. 'Believe me, I *felt* like wringing your neck when I first walked in. I don't take kindly to people thinking they can make use of my staff as and when the need arises, just because I've said I'll consider doing business with them.'

Rebel stared upwards in dismay. 'You thought I got Steve to help me because I knew he was one of *your* employees?' she questioned, aghast.

'Didn't you?'

'No!' She shook her head vehemently. 'I had no idea who he worked for until he called you boss! When he arrived he just said he'd come in from some paddock or the other. I hadn't a clue whose property it was on.'

Chayne brought them to a halt as he began shaking with laughter, and cupped her face between his hands. 'Then I do apologise, most humbly,' he offered with a ruefully shaped smile. 'You see, I believed you knew, all too well, just who employed him.'

Momentarily, it was all Rebel could do to rid herself of the stupid notion of wanting to throw her arms around his neck and kiss him. Dear lord, did he have to look at her in quite that heart-stopping manner? Eventually, by dragging her intoxicated gaze away and fastening it to his chest instead, she managed to clamp a brake on her unruly feelings.

'Oh, no, I didn't know,' she murmured throatily. Flicking him an apologetic glance of her own, she went on to grant, 'Although I am sorry for keeping him away from his work for so long.' Even if it hadn't entirely been her fault. 'I guess I should have known better, no matter whose employee he might have been.' Abruptly, her eyes flew worriedly to his and stayed riveted there this time. 'You didn't fire him, did you?'

A hand sliding to the nape of her neck turned her head slightly to the right so she could focus on a group of four or five young men talking together, and she recognised Steve as being one of them.

'No, his wings may have been clipped somewhat, but he's still around,' came the wry-sounding admission.

'I'm glad,' she smiled earnestly, and hastily redirected her vision on finding a pair of rancorous blue eyes raking over her as Karina sailed past them. 'I—I liked him, and he was very obliging.'

They started moving again themselves now. 'Oh, yes, I'm sure he was,' Chayne averred, lightly sarcastic. 'Only don't expect to be seeing him in town again during the day for quite some time to come, hmm?'

'It's off limits?'

'He's lost his wheels!'

'I'm sorry?' she frowned.

'The bike,' he elucidated laconically. 'The next time he's sent down to check the water tanks he'll be doing it the long, hard, hot way ... on horseback. A few weeks of that might help remind him where his priorities lay.'

Poor Steve! Rebel spared him some moments of sympathy before half laughing, 'Mmm, Van said it wasn't as pleasant and easy as it looks!' Her glance turned quizzical as the remark jogged her memory. 'Why didn't you tell me you were Van's employer during his time as a stockman?'

The crowd on the floor was becoming thicker by the minute and Chayne drew her protectively nearer. 'I thought you may have started asking questions I would, at the time, rather not have answered.'

'In case it meant you revealing something about his drinking, you mean?' Without waiting for his reply she immediately protested, 'Don't you think it would have been kinder to have told me what was going on, instead of leaving me to stumble into it unprepared?'

'So what could you have done if we had told you? Worried about it for an extra two days? What would have been kinder about that? We figured you were going to find out soon enough.'

Rebel's head tilted to one side, her expression one of suspicion tempered with humour. 'Are you sure you and Murray haven't rehearsed this together? You sound just like a tape recording of him from yesterday afternoon,' she retorted drily.

'I'm sure,' he laughed. 'I haven't even seen him since Tuesday evening.'

'Then I suppose ...' She broke off, frowning, as her attention was distracted by two men near the doorway who looked as if they had just arrived. One in his fifties, the other some thirty years younger, it was the older man who appeared to be signalling them, and in smiling mime she pointed to Chayne to see if that was who they did, in fact, require. The younger man immediately grinned and held up a thumb and forefinger in a circle of approval.

'What in blazes are you doing?' Chayne demanded in a lazy drawl.

'Making assignations on your behalf,' she twinkled. 'There's a couple of men behind you desirous of catching your eye, I believe.'

'Oh?' He spun them around so he could see for himself, a pleasurable smile lighting his features on recognition 'C.K. ... and Randall!' An arm was looped across her shoulders and she found herself being shepherded towards the doorway. 'Come on, and I'll introduce you. You'll like Randall, he's the daredevil in the family.'

'He's your brother?' With the age difference between him and Scott she had wondered if perhaps there weren't more in the family.

'Uh-huh! He's number four of six.'

The arch of her brows reached their highest peak. 'You mean, you've got *six* brothers?' She hadn't anticipated *that* many!

'Mmm, but no sisters, though,' he grinned at the astonishment in her tone.

'And C.K.?' she asked faintly.

'He's my father,' he furnished mockingly, his eyes shining with a taunting glint. 'Or were you of the opinion I didn't have one?'

She sent him an audacious sidelong look from the cover of dusky lashes. 'I must admit the thought did cross my mind this afternoon,' she ventured impudently.

'You'll keep!' His retaliation was only lazily voiced, but it succeeded in creating a feeling of shivery apprehension within her all the same.

CHAPTER SEVEN

No sooner had Rebel made the acquaintance of Chayne's father and brother—both of whom she found herself warming to immediately—than Scott appeared out of nowhere, together with another two brothers and their wives. It was obviously some time since any of them had seen Randall and his unexpected appearance at the dance was greeted with a great deal of pleasure, as well as goodnatured raillery.

Harland, the second oldest of the brothers as far as Rebel could make out, was the first to speak once the salutations and welcoming handshakes had been dispensed with.

'Hey, I thought you said you intended spending a few weeks at a mate's property in the Territory, and that you wouldn't be home for Christmas,' he puzzled.

'That was the general idea,' Randall conceded with a grin. 'Until I discovered his sister was hearing wedding bells every time we met. Then, deciding discretion was the better part of valour, I invented an urgent need for a major overhaul on the chopper and got myself out of there as fast as was humanly possible.'

Amid the general laughter which followed this disclosure, Chayne relayed in an aside for Rebel's benefit, 'Randall owns a helicopter and goes aerial mustering in the Northern Territory for seven months of the year during the dry season. Now that the wet's arrived—or the "green season" as they prefer it called these days—he was planning to take a month or so off before heading south.'

'Only his plans went a little awry,' she chuckled softly, then whispered back, 'And Harland and Eaton, they live around here, do they?'

He nodded. 'Harland's got a place on the other side of Deep Wells, and Eaton has one at Castlefield.'

Under cover of the roasting Scott was now giving his brother, Rebel sought to find out more about the family. 'Your other two brothers, are they likely to turn up later too?'

'I shouldn't think so. As far as I know they're still in Sydney and Perth respectively.'

'They're not graziers, then?'

'No,' Chayne shook his head and smiled. 'Linden's an airline pilot, and Jason's a research scientist with the Department of Agriculture.'

'Are they married?' To date, two out of seven wasn't much of an average.

'Linden is, but Jason reckons he subscribes to Randall's theory where marriage is concerned,' he grinned.

'Oh, and what's that?' she half laughed, half frowned.

In lieu of answering he indicated with his head that she should listen to Randall as he expounded affably in response to Eaton's laughing query as to whether he ever intended relinquishing his single status, 'Not me, old son. I still firmly adhere to the true bachelor's motto that it's better to go through life wanting something you haven't got than to discover you've got something you don't want! Besides, let's be honest,' his good-looking face creased in a broad smile, 'I'd be hell to live with.'

He had four brothers who were all too willing to attest to that statement, and who did so without hesitation, but once their bantering candour ceased and they began to talk of other matters, Rebel became increasingly conscious that this was a family gathering and that she was the odd one out. A feeling which was in no way lessened when Karina confidently positioned herself on Chayne's other side and linked her arm possessively with his.

'Darling, you should have sent Rebel to tell me what a surprise Randall had sprung on us,' she scolded archly. 'The poor girl looks most uncomfortable, and I'm sure it's only because she feels quite out of her depth hearing you talk about matters and people she knows absolutely nothing about.' A sweetly malicious smile was directed towards the younger girl. 'You would much prefer to be with people with whom you have something in common, wouldn't you, Rebel?'

If she hadn't felt out of place before, Karina had certainly seen to it that she did now, and hunching one shoulder embarrassingly she encompassed them all with a tight little smile.

'Yes, well, I must admit I was intending to look for my brother, so if you'll all excuse me . . .?' And without giving anyone a chance to speak, or perhaps detain her, she spun on her heel and walked speedily away.

When an encircling glance of the hall didn't bring any sign of Van to light she came to a halt, wondering if she should continue looking for him outside or not. She didn't want to appear to be checking up on him! Someone catching at her arm suddenly made the decision for her.

'Hi! Have you met everyone yet?' she found Denise enquiring of her sociably.

'Well, no, not really, I . . .'

'Oh, isn't that just like a man, to bring you to a gathering like this and then leave you to fend for yourself!' Denise cut in, part amused, part annoyed, and began guiding Rebel along with her. 'Never mind, though, you come with me and we'll soon remedy that.'

And in no time at all it seemed to Rebel that she had been taken around and introduced to just about everyone in town, as well as quite a number from the surrounding district.

'There, that's better,' smiled the older girl as they made their way back to the group they had started with. 'At least you'll have some idea now as to who's who.'

'But only if you keep prompting me,' laughed Rebel. 'I seem to be recalling a tremendous number of faces I can't put names to.'

'Oh, it won't be long for you to remember them all, and especially if you're going to be working in the store. In fact, you'll probably get like the rest of us before too long,' wryly.

'In what way?'

'Wishing you *could* forget some!' Denise grinned broadly.

Where the Lamberts were concerned Rebel felt that way already! She had just renewed her acquaintance with Sharon and it had left her no more attracted to the girl than she had been before. As to her parents—well, they hadn't really come across as the most friendly and hospitable couple on earth either, so perhaps it wasn't surprising their offspring were like they were.

Immediately they rejoined the gathering of her friends, however, Denise's smile faded and she searched their now less than gay expressions curiously.

'For heaven's sake, what happened while we were away?' she queried, nonplussed. 'You all look as if you've lost fifty dollars and found five cents.'

'We just heard that Lillian Knowles had to be taken to hospital today with an arm and two ribs broken,' Greg Balfour, the intending bridegroom Murray had pointed out to Rebel earlier, took it on himself to explain. 'Apparently she slipped and fell on a wet floor.'

'Oh, that's a shame,' Denise frowned. 'Although at her age I suppose it could have been a lot worse. She must be sixty-five, at least.' She glanced round the circle again. 'There aren't complications, are there?' Alarm in her voice now in view of their still doleful faces.

'Not unless you take my wedding cake into consideration,' put forward Wendy glumly.

Denise clapped a hand to her forehead in understanding.

'Of course! She was going to decorate it for you, wasn't she? I gather it's not finished.'

'It's not even started yet.' Wendy gave a dismal sniff. 'She was going to come over and do it this week.'

'You've got the cake, so why not take it to Deep Wells and have it decorated in there?' suggested Jocelyn Wymer practically.

Wendy didn't look at all taken with the idea. 'Sandra Beattie did that when she got married, and you know what a mess her cake looked by the time they got it back out here.'

'Well, there must be *someone* else besides Lillian who can do all those fancy trimmings. What about that girl over at Castlefield?' Denise proposed, and began clicking her fingers as she tried to remember. 'Oh, damn! What's her name?'

'If you mean Rita Hagan, she's gone down to relatives in Adelaide for Christmas,' Jocelyn divulged flatly.

In the silence which followed Rebel hunched one shoulder and made a diffident offer. 'I could do it for you, if you like.'

'You mean it? You can really do all that piping, and make roses, and everything?' Wendy's face came alive with glowing animation.

A selfconscious nod, and then Jocelyn was demanding in typically forthright fashion, 'Then for crying out loud, why didn't you say so earlier?'

'Because I didn't want to look as if I was pushing myself in if there was someone else Wendy would rather have do it.'

'Huh!' the postmistress snorted wryly. 'As you've just heard, there isn't *anyone* else here who can do it. You've just been elected, my girl.'

'Luckily for me!' exclaimed Wendy joyfully. 'Oh, Rebel, I don't know how to thank you. I was so disappointed at the thought of not having a proper wedding cake.'

'You don't have to thank me,' Rebel disclaimed self-effacingly. 'I enjoy doing them. I used to do a lot for my aunt's friends when I was in Adelaide.' She didn't also add that after her aunt had taught her the art—and she became more proficient than her teacher—Aunt Enid used to like to claim her niece's work as her own. 'How far has the cake actually progressed?'

'Mum put the marzipan on yesterday. Lillian said she always likes that on a few days before she starts to ice them.'

Rebel did some rapid mental calculations. 'In that case, I guess I'd better come out on Sunday to give it its first coat of royal icing, its second on Tuesday, and decorate on Thursday and Friday. How many tiers are there?'

'Three.'

'And you've got the boards for each one, and the silver paper, supporting columns, tulle, and ribbon?'

'Oh, no, they're all over at Lillian's. She was going to bring them over when she came,' was the worried disclosure. Wendy turned to her fiancé with a cajoling look. 'But Greg will drive over there tomorrow and collect them, won't you, love?'

'Do I get a choice?' he quizzed drily, resignedly.

She beamed him a smile and shook her head expressively.

'I hope we can borrow her piping bag and nozzles too,' put in Rebel anxiously. 'Unfortunately, I don't have any with me.'

'I'll give her a ring at the hospital tomorrow to find out, but I'm sure she won't object.' Wendy wasn't going to allow anything to dampen her hopes now. 'And for the sake of . . .' She broke off as another two joined the assembly, her baby blue eyes shining excitedly at the sight of the second figure. 'Randall! When did you get back? How long are you staying? Will you still be here for my wedding next Saturday?'

Randall laughed and replied just as rapidly. 'Late this afternoon. I haven't made up my mind yet. Yes, I will be here.'

The other new arrival, whose presence Rebel had been deliberately ignoring, now fixed the vivacious brunette with a sobering gaze. 'Did you hear that Lillian Knowles had broken her arm, though, Wendy?' asked Chayne sympathetically. 'I'm afraid she won't be able to do your cake now, you know.'

'No, I realise that.' Some of Wendy's excitement dimmed at the thought of the mishap which had occurred, although it was impossible to keep all her elation under control as she bubbled, 'But Rebel's said she can do it for me instead! Isn't that fortunate?'

'Very,' he agreed laconically, his eyes surveying the fiery-coloured curls on the downbent head of the girl beside him. 'I wouldn't have thought you'd be able to drag her away from the store for a week.'

Those same copper tendrils were now tossed back in an agitated movement as Rebel at last acknowledged his presence, but with narrowing eyes. 'What do you mean, drag me away from the store for a week?' she demanded suspiciously.

Wendy was only too eager to explain. 'Well, we couldn't possibly expect you to make the trip out there and back four or five times in the one week, you'd spend all your time travelling. Lillian was going to stay right until the wedding,' she added as if that settled the matter. 'In fact, that's what I was about to say when Chayne and Randall arrived. For the sake of one day—seeing you said you'd be starting on Sunday—I was going to suggest that you may as well come back with us tonight and save yourself the trouble of driving out. Unless you know where all the good and bad spots are in the road, it can be an extremely trying journey for visitors.'

'Makes sense,' nodded Jocelyn sagely.

'But I can't leave the store for all that time,' Rebel protested, appalled. What with Van's uncaring attitude she could find all her good work undone by her return. Of course, the fact that it would also mean living in close proximity to the disturbing man next to her was totally incidental, she managed to convince herself righteously.

Denise, however, wasn't about to forget the outback's

unwritten law regarding helping one's neighbours—even if Rebel had—and she willingly offered her services with a deprecating smile. 'Oh, I can easily look after it for a week, if that's the only thing stopping you.'

'But I couldn't ask you to do that,' Rebel demurred. 'You've got your own family to look after, and especially now that your children are on holiday.'

'That's no bother. I'll just take them down with me and they can help too. They'll enjoy it.'

'Oh, good, it's all settled, then.' Wendy took it for granted. 'And you'll come back with us tonight?'

'I—I . . .' What could she say? That she was nervous of leaving Van on his own because she was frightened he might slip back into his old ways during her absence? That would only belittle him, and make her sound like a watchdog! 'All right, I'll stay for the week,' she surrendered defeatedly. 'But I won't go back with you tonight, thank you all the same. I'll drive out on Sunday. That will give me tomorrow to do my packing and check that everything's okay in the store.'

Fortunately, that seemed acceptable to everyone and the talk moved on to other matters related to the wedding preparations. But now that Chayne had arrived, Rebel found it disconcerting that her thoughts should keep wandering into dangerous areas she would preferred to have ignored and, using her brother as an excuse once again, she proffered her apologies and made to leave.

Her retreat was promptly cut off before it had hardly begun by Chayne catching hold of her arm. 'I believe I owe you an unfinished dance,' he drawled.

'Oh?' She looked pointedly to his other side, where she had last seen Karina clutching at him so proprietorially, and cast him a challenging glance. 'Are you allowed?' she gibed mockingly.

Sooty-framed eyes narrowed fractionally, warningly, but it was the indolent tilt shaping his firmly moulded lips which created most of Rebel's inward turmoil as his head neared hers.

'Would you care to retract that, honey, or would you prefer to have me demonstrate just how mistaken you are?' he baited.

Rebel's expression turned doubtful and she began chewing at a soft bottom lip. She was loath to give him an easy victory by having her withdraw the statement, yet he was far too unpredictable for her to dare risk the outcome if she didn't. Prudence eventually won out.

'Okay, so I was wrong,' she gave in somewhat less than gracefully. 'Now may I please leave?'

'Uh-uh, there's still that unfinished dance, remember?' he goaded, aggravatingly.

'And that's the way it's going to stay ... unfinished!' she flared, and unaccountably close to tears. He was shredding her emotions into tiny pieces on a mere whim! 'Why don't you stay in the big league where you belong, Chayne, and leave me alone? I don't like the games you play!' Jerking free of his grasp, she headed straight for the back door and hurried outside.

As she plunged from the bright interior of the hall into the murky darkness beyond the doorway her footsteps slowed, waiting for her eyes to become accustomed to the faint light being emitted by a crescent-shaped moon. Apart from the monotonous drone of insects and the whirring of Christmas beetles' wings as they divebombed any source of light in their annual hordes, it was almost deathly silent once she moved away from the building. Then, far in the distance, a marauding dingo—that strange, wild, barkless dog—howled hauntingly to others of its kind, the sound lingering uncannily in the quiet still air and sending prickles of unease down her spine.

With an unconscious shiver she rounded the corner of the hall, wondering if one of the voices she had suddenly detected could belong to Van. It was too late to turn back when she discovered that he wasn't a member of the trio she had stumbled upon, but that the two Lambert brothers were.

'Got tired of them fancy squatters in there and came to

find yourself some real men, did you?' leered Walter unpleasantly.

Rebel took a couple of paces backwards and directed her gaze towards Morris, who she considered the least objectionable of the two. 'No, I was looking for Van, actually. Have you seen him?'

'Sure! Down the pub.' It was Walter who answered with a raucous laugh. 'He's probably as full as a boot by now.'

'I see,' she nodded as impassively as possible, reluctant to let them guess how depressed the news made her feel. 'Thank you.'

As she prepared to skirt round them Walter grabbed at her shoulder, causing her to lose her balance and lurch against him. 'What's your rush? You'll never get old Van out of there now, he's set for a session,' he told her sneeringly, his arms wrapping about her tightly. 'And with him drinking whatever you make, you'd better start thinking about being real nice to me if you want to keep that store.'

All Rebel's disappointment disappeared beneath an overwhelming anger aimed at the whole male sex. 'Nice to you?' she spat at him scornfully, and struggling furiously against the bands which kept her arms pinned to her sides. 'I wouldn't be nice to you if my life depended on it, you contemptible blackmailing scum!'

'We'll just see about that!' he ground out balefully as he sank a hand roughly within her hair, immobilising her head.

'*Walt!* Leave her alone!' Once again Morris intervened warningly.

'Yes, *Walt*, you'd do well to listen to your brother!' Chayne's voice recommended icily from out of the darkness, just before his hand grasped hold of Walter's hair and snapped his head back with a ferociousness that should have broken his neck. '*Leave her alone!*'

With a grunt of pain and anger, the younger Lambert involuntarily released Rebel, then swung round to face his assailant, all in the one movement.

'All right, Cavanagh, you asked for it!' he snarled, one clenched fist flashing out with murderous intent.

To Rebel's relief that alert suppleness of Chayne's proved to be no illusion. He dodged, agilely, then hammered a fist into Walter's mid-section which had that man doubling over and expelling his breath in a pained gasp. Before he could recover, Chayne had hit him again, a punishing blow to the side of the jaw this time which sent Walter crashing to the ground ... out cold and outclassed!

It all happened with such numbing swiftness that for a time no one moved. Then Chayne glanced over at Morris, hard-eyed and watchful, his loose-limbed stance more significant than words.

'Not me, feller!' Morris denied with a laugh that was half rueful, half disgusted. 'I'm not fighting my brother's battles for him. If he gets done in a scrap he starts, that's his look-out.'

'What's going on? And who's that on the ground?' no one had noticed Van's approach until he stood before them, swaying slightly, and squinting at each of them in turn. 'Have I missed something?'

'Not much,' Chayne bit out, coldly sarcastic. 'Just Walt's attempts to force his attentions on your sister.'

'Oh, God!' Even in the pale light it was possible to see Van's features turn ashen. 'I'm sorry, Reb.'

'So am I, Van,' she whispered throatily. 'Sorry that your word obviously means nothing to you. Couldn't you have stayed away from the hotel for *one* night?' Her voice broke disconsolately.

Walter began climbing groggily to his feet, with the aid of his brother and companion, but his temporary period of insensibility didn't appear to have improved his disposition at all, for he immediately began to threaten over his shoulder as they prepared to lead him away, 'I'll get you for this, Cavanagh, you see if I don't! You haven't seen the last of me by a long shot! As for you ...' his attention focussed on Rebel, 'there'll be other times when he's not around, you mark my words!'

Chayne stiffened, smothering an epithet. 'Get him out of here, Morris, or so help me ...!'

'Okay, okay!' Morris threw up an appeasing hand. And to his brother, 'Shut up, you bloody fool! Your mouth's caused enough trouble already!'

As they started to leave Rebel remembered she had some gratitude to express and she eyed the taut figure beside her selfconsciously. After all, it wasn't so long ago that she had fractiously walked out on him.

'Thank you for your—um—timely intervention,' she murmured awkwardly. 'I don't know what I would have done if you hadn't stepped in like you did.'

'Is that supposed to be a dig at me?' demanded Van aggressively, chin outthrust.

It hadn't been, but after tonight's events she was in no mood to considerately pamper his feelings. 'If you want to see it that way, why not? It seems fairly appropriate!' she retaliated tartly.

He gave a contemptuous snort, his eyes searching skywards. 'And to think I was looking forward to you joining me! I didn't know I'd be saddling myself with a whining, nagging killjoy! You should have stayed in Adelaide with Aunt Enid and Uncle Roger. The three of you must have been in your element together!'

Rebel stared at him in disbelief, her nails digging into her palms, her feelings lacerated by his denouncement, and her pride in a state of revolt because he had chosen to make it in public. Apart from Chayne, the Lamberts still hadn't moved completely out of earshot, and they were probably listening with avid interest.

'Well, at least I don't drop my bundle and start hitting the bottle at the first sign of disillusionment!' she slated witheringly. 'And if you want me out, then I'll go willingly, because there's no way I'll let you drag me down with you. I'm a fighter, Van, not a jellyfish! *One* of those is enough for any family, wouldn't you say?'

'Yeah! So's a wet blanket!'

A hard lump of anguish settled in her throat and, with a despairing shake of her head, she whirled and stumbled away. She wouldn't have believed it possible that either of them could have railed at the other so acrimoniously, and her one desire now was to escape the mortifying scene.

'I'll take you home so you can pack.'

Rebel's eyes were bitter as they ranged over Chayne keeping pace beside her, but her head was tilted defensively high. 'You're even more anxious to get rid of me than he is,' she gibed with desolating flippancy.

'Don't be a fool!' His retort was prompt and roughly voiced. 'I meant, so you could come back to Mount Cavanagh this evening.'

'Oh, yes, the wedding cake,' she recalled, an enormous effort required to keep her tone light and uncaring. 'I can't let Wendy down, can I? I guess Van will just have to wait another week before being able to sigh with relief at seeing the last of me.'

'Of course he doesn't want to see the last of you!'

'No?' she countered sardonically. 'It certainly sounded like it to me. You heard him say I should have stayed in Adelaide with—with ...' she almost lost the tight control she was exercising, but just managed to regain it in time to conclude stiffly, 'our aunt and uncle.'

'Yes, I heard him,' he had no option but to agree, albeit somewhat tersely. 'But that doesn't mean he believed it. He'd been drinking and probably hadn't a clue what he was saying. By morning, I doubt he'll even be able to remember what the argument was about.'

'Well, isn't that nice for him?' she jeered. 'Unfortunately, *I* won't have that advantage.' Pausing, she sent him a derisive glance. 'Anyway, how come you're defending him so diligently? Another case of the brave males of the species having to join forces in order to present a united front against a poor uncomprehending female?'

He shrugged one shoulder expressively. 'Someone has to put things in perspective, you're obviously not about to try. Perhaps in a week's time you'll have both cooled down ... and come to your senses.'

'So that we can *then* say goodbye to each other in

a properly civilised and adult m-manner?' she quipped shakily.

Chayne raked long fingers through his hair in exasperation. 'Damn you, Rebel, will you stop tearing yourself to pieces like that!' he ordered explosively. 'If you want to cry then damn well go ahead, but don't keep it penned inside you as you're doing! Your nerves are strung so tightly I can almost feel them quivering from here.'

'H-how annoying for you.' She attempted to laugh, but when it began to waver in the middle, hurried on to deny determinedly, 'But I have no reason to cry. I'm ...'

'Then perhaps someone should give you one!' he rasped grimly as he caught her to him and captured her lips in a harshly abrasive kiss.

It was the last thing she had been expecting, and although it did serve to banish every thought of her brother from her mind, the emotions it brought blazing into turbulent life were even more tormenting, and she fought to break free from his overpowering touch in frantic alarm.

Chayne merely cupped the back of her head with an inescapably strong hand and held her closer to his rugged frame while his mouth continued its ravaging assault, both on her lips and her senses. In the end she stopped struggling because she was just too tired and dispirited to battle against his dominance as well as the response she so recklessly found herself wanting to give. But the minute she ceased to strain away from him and her defences relaxed, the tears welled unbidden beneath her closed eyelids to course down her cheeks as she sighed out her submission between softly trembling lips.

When Chayne at last raised his head, it was only marginally, for his mouth lingered to sensuously kiss the salty dampness from her sweetly scented skin. In an agony of inflamed desire Rebel tore herself out of his arms, her breath coming in ragged, uneven gasps.

'All right, so you made me cry! Now are you satisfied?' Still wet eyes lifted to his insolently.

With a stifled oath he gripped hold of her arm and began marching her down the street. 'No, but the day's coming,' he grated incisively.

'Well, what did you expect me to say? Thank you?'

Halting them as suddenly as he had started them on their way, he swung her around to face him, his eyes keenly assessing as they roamed from her eyes which were filling with tears and confusion, to the lips she was chewing at so disconcertedly. Then he exhaled heavily and moved his head in an expression of incredulousness.

'Oh, hell! I must be out of my mind!' he laughed mirthlessly. 'You're so damned naïve and unaware that you're a danger to yourself, let alone anyone else!'

'Then go and play your oh, so sophisticated games with Karina! I'm sure she must be mature and aware enough even to suit you!' she cried brokenly, backing away. 'I apologise for falling so far short of your and Van's worldly ideals, but I didn't ask you to take me back to the store just now, it was your idea! Between the pair of you, and that revolting Walter Lambert, I've had enough of men for one evening, and if that makes me childish I don't damn well care, because I wish I'd never come here!'

On a choking sob she spun about and began running across the road, but as she reached the centre one of her high-heeled sandals slid on a rock, twisting her foot, and making her lose her footing so that she tumbled sideways on to the dusty surface. Too disgusted and despondent to move, she sat where she was, partially cross-legged, head bent, and massaging her newly tender ankle.

Chayne crossed to her swiftly and sank agilely down on to his haunches beside her. 'Are you hurt?' he asked of the top of her head. It was lowered so far he couldn't see anything of her face.

'No ... thank you,' she sighed in a small voice, but without looking up.

When a few seconds had elapsed and she had still made no effort to stand a purposeful hand beneath her chin made

certain he could scrutinise her forlorn features. 'You do
realise you're sitting in the middle of the road, don't you?'
he reminded her drily.

'Another childish characteristic of mine,' she flouted
dolefully with a sniff.

'Oh, honey, what am I going to do with you?' He started
to laugh wryly and, releasing her chin, lifted her to her
feet as he rose upright. 'Okay, I promise, no more games.
I shall be as circumspect and as proper as you could wish
from here on. Now will you stop looking so aggrieved and
go and pack?'

Rebel gave a reluctant nod. Van would obviously be
pleased to be relieved of her presence—he had made it all
too clear he regretted her arrival—so she supposed there
was no reason to stay in Pitereeka for that extra day. She
had no intention of forcing herself where she wasn't wanted,
and once the wedding was over she would be seeing about
returning to Adelaide. The troubling questions of where
she would live and what she would do once she got there
she determinedly put to the back of her mind. They were
problems she would solve when she came to them. At the
moment she already had more than enough to occupy her
thoughts.

And not the least of these disturbing thoughts was that
now Chayne had given his word to cease his discomfiting
provocations, contrarily, she found herself feeling somewhat depressed rather than consoled by the knowledge. A
circumstance she stoutly sought to reverse by reminding
herself that if one didn't want one's fingers burnt, one
didn't play with fire! For in view of her past emotional
responses there was no doubt in her mind that, with very
little effort on his part, Chayne Cavanagh could become an
all-consuming holocaust where she was concerned if she
didn't exercise extreme caution.

CHAPTER EIGHT

WITH her case packed and deposited in a silver-blue station wagon parked in the hall grounds, Rebel returned to the festivities in some trepidation, but as neither her brother nor the Lamberts were visible within the building, and their absence continued for the remainder of the evening, she was gradually able to relax a little. Van's less than sober denunciation had come so unexpectedly and so rancorously that it was doubtful she could have faced him with anything even approaching equanimity again that night, and as for the Lamberts ... well, if she never saw them again she would count herself lucky.

Wendy was delighted she had changed her mind and had decided to accompany them home after all, although Rebel didn't elaborate on her reasons for the alteration. She merely made the excuse that it hadn't occurred to her previously that if she drove herself out to Mount Cavanagh it would mean Van would be without a vehicle while she was away as he only had the one.

When it came time to leave there were four cars making the return trip to the property, and after Karina had finally said her coy and protracted goodbyes to Chayne, Rebel discovered herself to be sharing the front of the silver-blue wagon with him while the Metcalfes occupied the rear. It wasn't an arrangement she actually relished, but without drawing undue attention to herself there wasn't much she could do about it. The other vehicles were already filled with the remaining members of the Cavanagh family and their staff.

The first half hour or so of the journey was taken up with recollections by the other four passengers of reacquaintances made and the news they had to impart, together with various incidents which had occurred during

135

the evening. Rebel noted thankfully that there were none concerning either the episode with Walter Lambert or her argument with Van. She really wouldn't have liked either of them to become the subject of common gossip.

One by one, however, the voices quietened as the late hour and the soporific movement of the smooth-running vehicle combined to induce stifled yawns and heavily eyelids in all of them except, fortunately, their seemingly indefatigable driver. They were beginning to wind around the base of Mount Cavanagh itself now, and although Rebel would have liked to have seen what she could of the changing scenery as they began heading into those rolling ranges, her eyes kept closing for increasingly longer periods until she too slipped inexorably into sleep, the same as the three in the back. A couple of times a particularly heavier jolt than usual caused by the road's surface would bring her back to half consciousness, but as soon as the tyres resumed their rhythmic thrumming or less jarring sections she promptly reverted to her slumbers.

When she finally awoke, drowsily, it was to open her eyes slowly, and then blink them wide in astonishment to see light instead of darkness, and to suddenly realise she was in bed in a strange room and not still in a vehicle. Someone had considerately removed her dress and shoes before pulling up the sheet to cover her, but a slightly rueful grimace began to tug at her lips at the thought of inconveniencing her hostess to the extent of her having to put her to bed.

Sitting up, she swung her legs to the floor and looked about her with interest. It was a large attractive room with dark-stained and exposed beams dissecting the ceiling, the white walls adorned with a series of black-framed pen and ink sketches of well-known landmarks. The starkness of the colour scheme was relieved by the rich emerald green and the quilted cover which had been turned back at the foot of the bed and the matching floor-length curtains at the windows. The furniture had a heavy look about it which complemented the décor, and was as highly polished as the

gleaming parquetry floor. All things considered, she swiftly
came to the wry conclusion, it definitely was not how she
had imagined an overseer's cottage would look!

Her case was standing at the foot of the bed and, opening
it, she began rifling through its contents for her toiletries
and housecoat. These located, she slipped into the housecoat and picking up the deep green towel which had been
left on the dressing table headed for the door. Outside, she
found herself about halfway along a hall which had a
number of doors leading from it, and for a moment she
hesitated indecisively. Which was the bathroom? There
was only one door open, a little to her right on the other
side of the passage, but as she could plainly see it was another bedroom it didn't help her much. She couldn't just
go blundering along opening all of them until she came to
the right one, there was no telling what embarrassment she
might cause—for herself and others.

Suddenly, from across the way appeared the totally un-
anticipated but motherly figure of Doris Platt, the Cavanaghs' housekeeper, whom she had met last night.

'Oh, you're awake, are you, dear?' she smiled kindly.
'You just tell me what you'd like for breakfast and I'll see
that it's ready for you by the time you're dressed.'

'Thank you,' Rebel smiled her own response mechani-
cally, even as her brows drew together in a frown. 'Where
am I?' she puzzled.

The older woman's brown eyes widened expressively.
'Why, at Mount Cavanagh, of course! Where did you
think you were?' she went on with a half laugh.

'Oh, I knew it was the property,' Rebel hastened to explain selfconsciously. 'It's just that I didn't expect—I wondered . . . *is* this Dan and Thelma's house?'

'Good gracious, no, child. This is the homestead.'

'But—but I thought . . .'

'Ah, of course!' Doris nodded her realisation, her face
becoming wreathed in a smile. 'I was forgetting you were
fast asleep when Chayne carried you in last night and we
put you to bed. You were under the impression you'd be

staying with Dan and Thelma, is that it?'

'Well, yes,' concurred Rebel stiltedly, uncomfortable at the thought of what that *we* put you to bed' might entail. 'I certainly didn't expect to be staying in the homestead, and—and I'm sorry you had to go to the trouble of putting me to bed. You should have woken me.'

'It was no trouble, dear, and it would have been a shame to wake you from such a deep sleep,' her apology was dismissed lightly. 'As for your being here, well, I believe Chayne was of the opinion it might be a little too crowded at Thelma's place once their other children start arriving later in the week—along with their respective husbands, wives, and children!'

'I see,' Rebel smiled faintly. 'Well, I hope it won't cause you any inconvenience my being here.'

'Heavens, no!' exclaimed Doris sincerely. 'One extra isn't going to make any difference, and it will make such a nice change to have a pretty girl in the house besides all those strapping young men.' Her eyes twinkled irrepressibly. 'I must admit, I do sometimes wish for some feminine support when I'm surrounded by six of them at the table each evening.'

'Six?' With what she had learnt about the family Rebel couldn't quite make the figures tally.

'Mmm, C.K., Chayne, Scott, and the three jackaroos. Now, with Randall home too, it will be seven,' Doris chuckled.

An understandably disconcerting situation to be sure, conceded Rebel drily. The thought that she was about to share it wasn't exactly encouraging either. 'There's no Mrs Cavanagh, then?'

'No, Venetia's been dead for almost twenty years now,' Doris recalled sadly. 'She was riding up to the Lookout one afternoon—she often used to go there just for the view— but the track wasn't nearly as good in those days as it is now and her mount lost its footing and they both went over the edge.' She sighed heavily. 'Oh, it was a tragic day, that one!'

'You must have been here a long time yourself,' put in Rebel hastily, hoping to divert the older woman's attention away from the distressing subject.

'Twenty-nine years, in actual fact. I came as a hard-headed—or at least I thought I was—young woman of twenty-two to be governess and mother's help to four, as there were then, of the most unruly but endearing scamps you have ever seen,' she revealed with a laugh of remembrance. 'Chayne was five at the time and just starting lessons with the School of the Air, but with Harland and Eaton still toddlers, and Linden a babe in arms, Venetia just couldn't manage all of them and supervise Chayne's schoolwork as well. As the years passed they became my family too, and when Venetia died I was able to manage the housekeeping and the schoolwork because we only had the three younger ones at home then, the other four were at school in Adelaide for most of the time. These days I can devote all my energies towards the housekeeping,' she concluded humorously.

'Except when thoughtless visitors prevent you,' Rebel referred to herself ruefully. 'I'm sorry for holding you up with all my questions.'

'There's no worry,' Doris waved the suggestion aside, smiling. 'Believe me, after helping to raise a family of seven boys, I'm quite capable of telling someone they're interrupting me, if the need arises.'

As much as she would have liked to have delved further into the Cavanaghs' past—or the past of one particular member, she admitted to herself with wry honesty—Rebel thought it best to bring the conversation to an end anyway. At the moment Doris apparently didn't mind answering her queries, but there was no guarantee that state of affairs would continue indefinitely. It might be wisest if she reserved the rest of them for another day.

'Well, I think I'd better be getting a move on, in any case,' she smiled apologetically. 'I don't know what time it is, I forgot to look when I took my watch off, but I have the distinct feeling I should have been up and showered long before this.'

'But you're here as a guest, dear. You sleep in if you want to. It doesn't matter if you're up at seven or eleven.'

'That's not what time it is now, is it? Eleven?' Blue eyes widened in horror.

'No, no, it's only nine-thirty,' Doris soothed. 'But you'd like me to start your breakfast for you, would you?'

'Only if you could tell me where the bathroom is first,' Rebel laughed. 'And only tea and toast, thank you.'

After showering and dressing in a pale green skirt and a darker green top, Rebel had breakfast in the kitchen instead of the dining room so she could chat to Doris as that woman went about her work, and also in order to look over the wedding cakes which Thelma had delivered to the homestead an hour or so earlier.

'I wonder if Wendy wants them with a matt icing or a slight gloss,' she mused contemplatively as she gave the three decreasing-sized cakes a judicious look.

'I wouldn't know.' Doris's plump shoulders rose in a shrug of ignorance. 'Although all the ones I've ever seen have had that matt look about them. Is gloss the "in" thing now in town?'

'Not really, but you do occasionally get orders for them. I always find it's safest to ask, just in case.' Easing away from the table, Rebel rose to her feet and took her used plates across to the dishwasher. 'After I've unpacked my case I might wander over and have a talk to her about it, see if she has any preferences for designs, etcetera,' she said over her shoulder, placing the china inside the machine as she had seen the housekeeper do. Dishwashers were new to her. 'Am I likely to find her at home, or have I missed her too by rising too late?' Up until now the only persons she had seen at all were Doris and two friendly native house-girls.

'No, I expect she'll be around somewhere, fussing over something or the other,' Doris revealed with a laugh. 'She's nearly driven her mother berserk these last couple of weeks making sure everything is just perfect for next Saturday. And there's no need to worry about unpacking, I had young Betty do that for you while you were having breakfast. Thelma's place is that way if you're intending to go over,' motioning towards the rear of the house. 'If you go out the back gate you'll find it about a hundred yards on your left.'

'Thank you,' Rebel smiled gratefully, both for the directions and for having her unpacking done for her. 'I'll see you later then.'

'Just remember lunch is at one, and if you're late you miss out,' called the housekeeper, eyes narrowing with feigned threats. Then she explained with a chuckle, 'It was the only way I could be sure seven young boys would make it to the table on time.'

'I won't be late,' vowed Rebel, about to push out through the gauze door. 'I feel badly enough as it is having been so tardy for breakfast.'

'Oh, there's no set time for that meal,' she was enlightened casually. 'Too much depends on what the men have lined up for the day. Sometimes they eat early, sometimes late.'

'How late is late?' for curiosity's sake.

'Between seven and eight usually, maybe even nine on rare occasions.'

Rebel nodded and closed the door behind her. She didn't ask how early, early was. She had the feeling she would rather not know. One conclusion she had reached, however, was that no one on Mount Cavanagh could possibly have been termed a late riser!

The coolness within the homestead produced by the eighteen-inch-thick sandstone walls and the wide shading verandah hadn't prepared Rebel for the blast of searing heat which hit her like the flames from an open furnace the minute she set foot into the sunlight, and drawing in a deep breath, she blew it out again expressively. Without a doubt this was the hottest day she had experienced since her arrival in the northern ranges.

From the top of her head to the soles of her feet she

could feel the sun burning, penetrating clear through to
her bones. She could even feel it in the air she took into her
lungs—dry, stifling, scorching. Fortunately, she had a warm
peach tint to her complexion which enabled her to take
exposure to the sun to a far greater degree than most redheads, but even so, on a day such as this she judged it best
not to linger too long beneath those blistering rays without
any protection for either her head or her skin, and she
hastened towards the back gate with only a sketchy impression of tall trees and artistically arranged borders in the
well-kept garden registering on her mind.

It was approaching lunch time when Rebel returned to the
homestead after having spent the rest of the morning in
company with the prospective bride, and as she hurried into
the welcome shade of the verandah she noticed Chayne's
father seated in a comfortably padded cane chair, reading
a four-day-old newspaper.

'Warm enough for you?' he enquired conversationally,
humorously, seeing her wipe away the drops of perspiration
which had gathered at her temples during her walk.

Her lips curved wryly. 'Just about. Is it always this hot
so early in the summer?'

'Just about,' he copied in such a dry tone that he had
Rebel catching at her breath in a suddenly tense throat.
He so closely resembled his eldest son when he spoke in
that manner that it was quite unsettling. 'Perhaps you would
care for a drink before lunch to cool you down a little. I'm
having one.' He indicated a tall glass filled with amber
liquid on the table beside him.

'Thank you. I'd like a glass of fruit juice if you have it,
please,' she requested shyly. She doubted if the contents
of his glass were as innocuous, but not being used to alcohol
she really didn't fancy anything stronger while she was so
warm.

It was only a matter of minutes before her preference had
been fulfilled from the leather-studded bar in the room

behind them and she accepted it appreciatively, taking the seat he pulled forward for her.

'It's very kind of you to allow me to stay here, Mr Cavanagh,' she smiled earnestly. 'I hope I'm not putting you to too much trouble.'

'C.K., please,' he amended gently. 'And you're not putting us to any trouble at all, I can assure you. Besides, I rather think it's we who should be thanking you.'

'For what?' She looked at him, half frowning.

'For being so generous with your time in order to help Wendy out of her difficulty, and for being willing to grace an almost all-male household with your presence.'

'Oh, no, it's my pleasure! It's the sort of thing that's always appealed to—to . . .' She stopped, blushing furiously as she remembered the last half of his sentence. 'I—I'm only referring to the cake decorating, of course!' she tried to assure him embarrassedly.

'Much to the disappointment and deflation of my sons, I'm sure,' he quipped whimsically.

Rebel's eyes rounded in dismay. 'Oh, I didn't mean to imply that I wasn't—that they weren't . . .' She was becoming more flustered and selfconscious by the minute and she took what she hoped would be a steadying breath. 'I mean, of course, I think all your sons are very pleasant, it's just that I didn't come here . . .'

'With a view to furthering their acquaintance?' he interposed helpfully.

'That's right,' she averred on a shuddering sigh of relief, glad to have finally had the matter settled satisfactorily.

He picked up his glass and cast her an amused glance over its rim. 'There was no call for you to have sounded so worried, you know. I did understand what you were originally trying to say, even though you . . .' his mouth curved slightly, 'inadvertently left your wording open to interpretation.'

'I see.' Rebel dropped her own mortified gaze to the glass she was holding tightly between slender fingers. No doubt he now thought her as immature as his son did. 'I just didn't want you to get the wrong impression, that's all,' she murmured lamely.

His smile was tolerant as it rested on her downbent head. 'I didn't.'

A particular nuance in his tone had her raising her eyes doubtfully to his. She hadn't, perhaps, been too emphatic in her refutation, had she? But there was no time for her to dwell on the matter because the air was abruptly rent by the swelling sound of engines—three earth-bound in the form of motorbikes, the other the distinctive whirring of a helicopter rotor—and both their interests were drawn to the open area between the homestead fence and the out-buildings.

The first to arrive was Randall in the helicopter, who after climbing out of the machine, tossed his dark glasses back on to the seat, removed his protective helmet, and proceeded to rake his fingers through his hair as he waited for the others. They weren't far behind him and as one headed towards the overseer's cottage, the remaining two slowed and, with Randall walking beside them, continued on to the fence where they dismounted in the shade of a blue-green-leaved bullock bush—which wasn't a bush at all, but a tree.

Rebel watched their approach covertly, her gaze way-wardly concentrating on the tallest of the three figures. They all looked hot—was it any wonder?—dishevelled, and . . . irritated?

C.K. moved forward on his chair. 'How did you go?' he asked crisply as soon as they were withing talking range.

Randall answered for all three of them. He grimaced explicitly and gave a thumbs-down sign.

A disgruntled sound and their father leant back again, forcefully. 'What will you do now? Check the north-western section?'

'Yes!' Chayne clipped the word out shortly. 'We'll cover every damned inch of it if we have to.'

By the deepening creases which were furrowing her brow it was plain the conversation was completely beyond Rebel's grasp and, seeing them, it was Scott who perched himself on the verandah rail in front of her to elucidate with a grin, 'You remember, I told you in Deep Wells that we were losing stock? Well, we still haven't been able to locate the exact areas of their operation as yet.'

The creases disappeared magically. Now she understood! But before she could give voice to her comprehension Chayne had erupted wrathfully.

'Are you mad?' he demanded of his brother. 'You knew damned well we'd decided not to say anything about this! What the hell did you think you were doing telling her, of all people?'

'Now wait just one minute!' Rebel wasn't going to let that go uncontested.

'Chayne!' cautioned his father with a frown.

'I couldn't see any harm in it,' Scott declared half defensively, half apologetically.

Randall grinned and made for the bar fridge.

'You couldn't see any harm in it!' Chayne repeated with sarcastic mimicry. 'With *her* connections?'

'I'm sorry, I didn't think,' conceded Scott wryly.

Rebel deposited her drink on the table with a thud and leapt to her feet, bristling. 'And just what do you mean ... *my* connections?' Blue eyes blazed irately into brown-flecked green.

'Anyone for a drink?' enquired Randall from the doorway, momentarily breaking the crackling atmosphere, and tossing a can of beer to each of his brothers before reefing back the tab on his own and sampling the brew appreciatively.

Refusing to be diverted from her purpose, Rebel returned her gaze to the man who was now leaning negligently against one of the verandah roof supports. 'Well?' she glared.

'In a single word—Van?' he retorted succinctly.

'Why, that's ridiculous! You couldn't possibly think he's got anything to do with it!' her protest was made with hot indignation. No matter what else he may have done

she couldn't believe her brother capable of deliberate stealing, but when there was no easing of Chayne's set expression some of her confidence deserted her, and she followed
it with a far less certain, 'Could you?'

'No one said him—personally!'

He sounded almost annoyed by the suggestion and that
only served to increase her confusion. 'Well—well . . . I just
don't understand,' she sighed helplessly.

From behind her C.K.'s voice came quietly. 'Chayne,
under the circumstances, don't you think . . .'

'No!' His son's rebuttal was definite, final. Then, to
Rebel, 'When he's been drinking I doubt your brother could
keep a secret if he tried! So it will only have needed you
to have mentioned something about this to him and all our
efforts are down the drain. Everyone in the district will
know what's going on, and we won't have a hope in hell of
catching them.'

'But I didn't tell him! I didn't tell anyone!' she exclaimed resentfully. 'In fact, I'd forgotten all about it until
Scott just reminded me.'

'You're positive?' he probed brusquely.

'Of course I'm positive! In case you happen to have forgotten, I had enough worries of my own to think about,
without taking on any of yours as well!'

'My God! I do believe you've created history, old son,'
Randall laughed across at his elder brother. 'You've found
a female who can keep a secret.'

Naturally enough the remark brought a smile to all the
male faces present, smiles which broadened when Chayne
reflected in mocking accents, 'But only, I gather, because it
had been temporarily displaced from her mind.'

Devastated by that fascinating smile of his, and unable
to ignore him as she would have liked, Rebel rounded on
him huffily. 'That's not fair! I can keep a secret as well as
any of you can!'

'Yes, I've no doubt you can.' It was C.K. who came to
her defence with an encouraging smile, rising to his feet.
'As for you three,' his eyes ranged over his sons sardoni-

cally, 'I suggest you devote your energies to getting cleaned up, otherwise you'll be late to the table, and Doris ...'

'Won't give you any lunch ... *I hope*!' smirked Rebel with a delighted chuckle of revenge as she accompanied C.K. to the doorway.

'Cat!' retaliated Chayne promptly to a chorus of gnashing teeth. 'Unlike some, we've been working out in that heat since six this morning. What time did you finally consent to leave *your* bed, honey?'

Briefly, she faltered, a selfconscious warmth flooding her cheeks, then she made a determined recovery. Having succeeded in turning the tables on him she wasn't going to squander the advantage.

'Oh, only about half an hour ago,' she handled the truth lightly, airily, before sending him a highly taunting glance. 'Without your scintillating company to entertain me, there just wasn't a reason to get up any earlier.'

She was already into the hall when the pungent comeback, 'Ho! That's easily fixed in future!' reached her ears, but from that distance she couldn't quite decipher which one of them had said it.

Some suspicions did enter her mind during lunch, however, when Randall suddenly caught her eye and recommended banteringly, 'If it's entertainment you want, why don't you hitch a ride with Chayne when we go back out this afternoon? His bike's got a double seat.'

He made it sound like a dare, and in the mood she was in Rebel was all too willing to accept it. 'All right, I will,' she stated brashly.

'No, you won't,' Chayne vetoed with a lazy shake of his head.

'Why not?' Her gaze turned disappointed.

'Oh, because you wouldn't like it, dear,' put in Doris from the end of the table. 'You'd find it most unpleasant with the heat, and the dust, and all that bouncing around.'

'Besides which, some sections are just too rough and dangerous to be taking you over them,' C.K. added his own reservations.

'And if that wasn't enough, there's sunburn, windburn, and an unavoidable assortment of grazes and scratches to be contended with as well. With your fair skin, honey ... uh-uh!' Chayne disallowed wryly.

Rebel tried for one last chance. 'I did keep your secret for you,' she reminded him with sly emphasis.

He just threw back his head and laughed, but before he could answer help began to appear from other quarters.

'Oh, go on, let her come,' urged Scott with a grin. 'A long-sleeved shirt, jeans, and boots, are all the clothes she needs for protection.'

'And a crash-hat with a visor will stop the sunburn and windburn,' Randall supplemented.

'While boiling her head inside it on a day like today!'

'But Randall wears one in the helicopter,' Rebel joined in.

'Not with a visor attached, he doesn't.'

'Oh, please, I don't mind, really,' she resorted to entreating, her eyes holding his valiantly. 'I would so like to see something of the area while I'm here, and if I don't see it this week, I never will!'

The men appeared to grow strangely quiet, and it was left to Doris to unwittingly demur, 'Of course you'll be able to see it another time, dear. Although I'd be more inclined to choose a time during winter, if I were you.'

Rebel nodded and smiled weakly. There was nothing to be gained from correcting Doris's misapprehension. She would find out soon enough anyway after next weekend.

'Okay, you can come,' Chayne unexpectedly relented, running a hand around the back of his neck and sighing.

She chewed at her lip doubtfully. 'You're sure?' Not even Scott and Randall seemed particularly enthusiastic now.

He smiled lazily, his eyes crinkling at the corners. 'I'm sure.'

'Th-thank you,' she acknowledged shakily, throatily, and dropped her gaze to her plate in self-preservation. When he looked at her in just that fashion all her defences annoyingly faded away and left her feeling far too vulnerable for comfort.

As Rebel hadn't brought either boots or a long-sleeved shirt with her, they borrowed these articles of clothing from Wendy who, fortunately, was of an approximate size. The crash-hat Scott dug out for her was a bright orange and settled snugly over her head, although she noticed as they headed through the garden that both Chayne and Scott retained the shading bush hats they had worn before lunch.

Swinging a long leg over the machine Chayne kicked it into roaring life and slanted her a quizzical glance. 'Ever ridden one before?'

'No.'

'Well, hop on.' He nodded towards the seat behind him, and when she had complied, continued, 'Put your feet there,' indicating the footrests, 'and keep your toes *up*, otherwise you're likely to lose a foot.'

'I'll keep them up,' she vowed with a gulp. 'What do I hold on to ... you?'

He flashed her a provoking smile. 'For preference. At least that way I can be certain you're still aboard.'

'Anything else I should know?' She fought to keep her voice light.

'Yes,' he turned to impress over a broad shoulder. 'When I lean with the bike, you make damn sure you lean with me, hmm?'

She nodded obediently and caught a firm grip on the leather belt about his lithe waist. After the persuasion which had been necessary to obtain his consent to take her, she meant to do everything in her power to see there wasn't one single thing he could complain about by the time they returned.

They met up with Dan Metcalfe on the third bike just beyond the woolshed and, with Randall preceding them in the air, they set off across the undulating grasslands towards a line of rocky foothills in the distance. The bikes travelled separately, of course, in order to avoid each other's dust, but the noise of their passing, combined with the helicopter overhead, was flushing out all manner of animal and bird life which kept Rebel gazing about her, fascinated.

Apart from the heavily woolled sheep which scattered in all directions at their approach, there were big red kangaroos to watch bounding effortlessly out of the way, and long-legged emus which kept pace with the bikes without any trouble at all, while less agile little quail darted deeper into the grass uttering squeaky calls of 'chip-chip-chip' in their alarm.

From clumps of trees, or lone timber sentinels, rose up harshly indignant flocks of birds. Sometimes white corellas, which didn't display their pretty yellow underwings until airborne; then there were the barred green and yellow bodies of the smaller, but extremely vociferous, budgerigar; and the colourful red-beaked zebra finches.

Slowly but surely they closed with those stony ridges and gullies, and with them a fence, which Rebel presumed to be a boundary as they turned and began following it. She had already discovered there wasn't much point in trying to ask questions of Chayne while they were moving, because even if he did manage to hear her queries which were muffled by the visor, then she found it impossible to hear his replies through the helmet and above the noises of the bikes.

The way was becoming a lot rougher now as they started twisting and weaving between bushes and rocks, across a gouged and dry watercourse, around fallen trees and broken stumps. They were still disturbing wildlife—rock wallabies, lizards, even a coiled snake—but Rebel couldn't afford to pay them too much attention any more as all her concentration was required now to ensure she didn't upset their balance on one of those jinking turns. Spiky grass and thorny bushes slapped viciously at their arms and legs as they dodged through the undergrowth, and she edged closer to that wide back in front of her for protection, her arms sliding further around him and her head ducking quickly as they suddenly swept beneath a gnarled branch of an old tree.

Chayne half turned his head, grinned, said something, but Rebel couldn't make out what it was, so she contented herself with a shake of her head and an answering smile, then went back to sheltering close behind him until at last they had cleared the crumbling sandstone outcrops and were cutting across mirage-producing saltbush flats where once the sea had ruled supreme.

If she had thought she was hot before, it was nothing compared to how she felt now as trickles of perspiration began to find their way down her spine and between her breasts. The hair clinging to the nape of her neck was wet through, as were the strands which had worked down on to her forehead and which she longed to be able to tuck out of the way. Ahead of them she could see lakes of cool blue water as well as groves of trees and, licking at dry lips with an almost as dry tongue, she smiled to herself ruefully. So it was true! Those shimmering waves of heat which danced and beckoned in the distance could play tricks on the eyes.

The next time Randall returned from one of his far-ranging surveys Chayne signalled him down, and as they started to slow themsevles Rebel gave a small sigh of gratitude. Although she was thoroughly enjoying the experience, she wouldn't be at all sorry to be able to remove her crash-hat for a while, or to change her position. She was beginning to feel just a little cramped.

No sooner had they come to a halt than she had dismounted, removed her headgear, and was combing her fingers through her decidedly damp hair—much as Randall did immediately he left the helicopter. Then she arched her back and proceeded to stretch her legs pleasurably.

'Think you'll be able to make the round journey?' Chayne quizzed wryly.

'Of course!' she retorted confidently, before her brows rose to an enquiring level. 'Does that mean we'll be heading back from here?'

'Uh-uh! From here we start to break new ground. We travel further north.'

'But whatever it is you're looking for, wouldn't Randall,' nodding to where he, together with Scott and Dan, was poring over a map, 'be able to find it quicker and easier on his own from the air?'

'Not necessarily, even if they use one of these open paddocks, which I doubt, but once we cut back into the ranges there are some gorges where he just doesn't have the room to manoeuvre as much as he needs to for this type of search, so we like to double check those areas on the bikes.'

Her lips pursed thoughtfully as she turned the matter over in her mind. 'But surely you know which paddocks you lost stock from, and that being the case, you must have some idea of at least the general area where you're likely to find ...' She paused and slanted him a questioning look. 'Just what sort of things are you looking for, anyway? Broken fences?'

'I wish it was that easy,' he owned ruefully. 'Unfortunately, however, these people are too professional for that. They've come prepared with loading ramps each time and haven't had to touch the fences at all.'

Loading ramps? 'You mean, they take them out in *truck* loads?' She had imagined them to be rounding up a few at a time on horseback and then driving them off into the sunset, as it were, not carting them away on road transports. That was one of the disadvantages of such a large property, she supposed. It was impossible to keep all of it under surveillance all of the time.

'They do,' he confirmed her startled query in staccato tones.

'Then if you know that, how come you don't know where they loaded them?' she puzzled.

'Oh, we know where they loaded them last time. What we're after at the moment is the point where they're *going* to load them next time.' He began moving towards the others.

For a few brief seconds Rebel stood exactly where she

was, nonplussed, and then she chased after him. 'Would you please explain that again, but preferably in such a way that I can understand it this time?' she requested sardonically. 'I mean, how do you know there's going to be a next time? And even if there is, how can you possibly hope to locate the area *prior* to it happening? What do you expect to find, a sign with a cross marked on it to mark the spot?' Sarcasm crept into her voice.

'Yeah,' he drawled facetiously, and resumed walking.

Rebel glared resentfully at his back and marched a pace or two behind him. 'All right, I'm sorry!' she flared quite unapologetically. 'But what else am I supposed to say if you won't actually come out and tell me what's going on?'

He halted, sighing heavily, his eyes turning skywards. 'God knows why I should tell you, because apart from C.K. not another person on the station besides the four of us here knows all the facts, but . . .' he shook his head incredulously, as if still unsure as to why he was about to be so communicative, 'both times before they've taken stock from the southern boundary paddocks, but we have reason to believe —the how and why of which need not concern you—they consider these more isolated north-western sections suit their purpose better, and that in order to make an even larger haul in the very near future they've already scouted the area and made their on site preparations.'

'And that's what you're looking for today?' Then, in a musing tone after his confirming nod, 'Scott said you had some suspicions as to who it might be. Have they been strengthened now?'

'Very much so since that flight down south,' he revealed sharply. 'We checked on some unsolved cases and found a couple of them fit the same pattern. A few head missing every now and again throughout the district over a period of a year or so, followed by successively larger mobs disappearing, and then nothing.'

'As if they'd moved on, you mean?'

'Mmm, that's the way it looks.'

They would have to have become very familiar with each

area then, to have been able to carry out their activities without detection, pondered Rebel to herself. So who were relative newcomers to Pitereeka and able to come by such knowledge? Dudley and Daisy Ruddock, the old couple who presumably went out prospecting each day, but never actually found anything? They would certainly have had the opportunity to get to know the surrounding properties, although try as she might, she really couldn't quite picture the harmless pair in the role of cattle thieves.

Apart from Van, whom she discounted immediately, the only other ones she knew who fitted the general description and had similar opportunities, were ... the Lamberts! Understandably, her own personal dislike of the family made it extremely easy to imagine them as the villains in the piece, but even after judiciously considering the matter from every angle she still couldn't escape her original thoughts. As contract fencers they had the perfect cover for such a venture.

She sent him a considering glance from the corner of her eye. 'I suppose the—er—Lamberts would get to know a place pretty well while they were out fencing, wouldn't they?' she insinuated tentatively.

'I guess they would at that,' he granted, the corners of his mouth tilting obliquely. 'Quite the little detective, aren't you, honey?'

'Aren't I, though?' she was quite agreeable to acceding, and flashed him a sparkling grin. 'Although I must admit I'm also a very hot and dry one at the moment. I don't suppose that blue lake I keep seeing out there is really filled with water, is it?'

He laughed. 'No, but the portable fridge in the chopper is, if you want a drink.'

'What? You mean I've been standing here talking all this time, when I could have been drinking? Oh, why didn't you tell me?'

'Because I naturally thought you would have preferred being entertained by my scintillating company,' he taunted.

Recognition feathered its way across her features and

she angled her head to one side as if considering the matter.
'No, I think I would have enjoyed a cold drink more,' she
quipped pertly, and prudently danced a few steps backwards.

Only she wasn't quite fast enough and a hand whipped
out to catch her by the nape of the neck before she could
escape. '*That* you are going to pay for before very long,'
Chayne threatened in a deeply timbred voice which had her
insides tying themselves in knots.

'So what are you going to do ... beat me again?' she
dared to challenge goadingly.

'Uh-huh!' he drawled his endorsement lazily. 'But this
time—at your own game!'

CHAPTER NINE

DURING the following days that enigmatic remark—threat?
—of Chayne's often resurfaced in Rebel's mind to cause her
some moments of perplexed disquiet, but so much else
seemed to be happening around the homestead that she had
very little chance to analyse it in any depth.

On Sunday morning, while she had been putting the
first coat of icing on the wedding cake, the men had finally
found what they had been searching for so diligently, and
which had frustratingly eluded them when Rebel had been
with them. Tyre tread marks where there shouldn't have
been any, running parallel to one of the most distant
paddocks, and leading into a stand of trees which had been
industriously encircled with two strands of wire, all ready
to be battery electrified as soon as the cattle had been driven
within. A very effective method of keeping them securely
penned while they were being loaded and very easy to erect
unobtrusively.

Since then Chayne had been in regular contact with

someone in Pitereeka, as well as someone else in Deep Wells, but this morning, Wednesday, a Land Rover had arrived just before lunch with two members of the police aboard, who were immediately whisked into the office and closeted there with the four Cavanaghs until meal time. To Rebel's disappointment their talk during lunch centred on anything except their reasons for being there—even though it wasn't difficult to guess—but when the men made for the Land Rover and Mount Cavanagh's Land Cruiser as soon as the meal was concluded, she knew without a doubt exactly where they were headed, and for what purpose.

With C.K. and Doris beside her, she watched sombrely from the verandah as they packed food and drinks into the vehicles—there could be a long wait ahead of them— her eyes never leaving one broad-shouldered, lean-hipped figure. She kept remembering Walter's menacing, 'I'll get you for this, Cavanagh!' from the night of the dance, and although she knew Chayne was only too well able to take care of himself, it made her go cold thinking of what someone like the younger Lambert might attempt when cornered.

Consequently, when Chayne returned to the homestead for something she followed him inside, and stood waiting nervously for him to re-emerge from his room. Immediately he did, her eyes sought his agitatedly, and in that instant she realised it wasn't just a well-intentioned anxiety which had sent her after him, but something far stronger. Somewhere, somehow, in the space of a little over a week, she had managed to lose her heart to this exciting, provoking, virile specimen of masculinity, and it was only the strength of that love which kept her facing him now, when all her protective instincts counselled a retreat.

Before her courage deserted her, and surrendering to an uncontrollable desire to touch him, she went up on her toes and laid a swift kiss against the bronzed skin of his cheek. 'Chayne, be careful,' she warned huskily.

For a brief moment an emotion Rebel couldn't quite identify flared deep within his eyes, then it was gone. 'I wasn't intending to be otherwise,' he drawled in a lightly teasing voice.

'But Walter Lambert may have other ideas about that,' she sought to impress on him worriedly, knowing it just wasn't in his nature to back off if the going got rough. 'He's got a grudge against you, Chayne, and I'm scared of what he'll do if he thinks he's got nothing to lose.'

Tanned fingers gently smoothed the curls back from her troubled forehead. 'Thank you for caring,' he smiled down at her softly. 'You're a sweet kid.'

Rebel could have cried with despair and frustration. She might have been inexperienced, but there was certainly nothing childlike in her feelings where this man was concerned, and the thought that he considered her so lacking in maturity was almost too much to bear. Next he'd be rumpling her hair as if she was his young sister, she forecast desolately.

From outside came the sound of a car horn which had them both automatically looking in that direction.

'I've got to go, honey,' Chayne sighed, and turned her face up to his with a hand beneath her chin. 'So stop looking so gloomy, hmm? Nothing's going to happen.'

'I—I hope not,' she attempted to smile, not wanting him to suspect that her dolefulness wasn't wholly attributable to his departure, but it wasn't very successful and she finished by catching her lip nervously between white teeth.

'Oh, hell!' He took a step forward and for one heart-stirring second she thought, hoped, he was going to kiss her. But, to her sorrow, he didn't. He gave a decisive shake of his head and pressed his lips together in an uncompromising line. 'I'll see you in the morning,' he advised flatly before turning on his heel and striding purposefully down the hall.

The vehicles were already on the move by the time Rebel had slowly made her way back to the verandah, and along with Chayne's father and the housekeeper, she watched them until they were lost to view behind the outbuildings, whereupon Doris returned inside.

'Will it go all right, do you think?' she asked tautly of C.K., although her eyes were still trained in the direction the vehicles had taken.

'I should think so, provided Van's information was correct.'

Van? She swung round quickly at that, her brows lowering in a frown. 'Do you mean my brother Van?' she puzzled incredulously.

'Er—yes, as a matter of fact, I do,' he smiled at her apologetically, a trifle uncomfortably. 'Although I'm sorry for letting the cat out of the bag. You caught me in an unguarded moment. They didn't want you to know until it was all over.'

'They?' she questioned rigidly.

'I would rather you waited until Chayne returned,' he evaded.

She eyed him part threateningly, part diffidently. 'Maybe I should go and ring Van and find out for myself.'

'You will not!' His voice fairly cracked with authority, but on seeing her stricken expression, he relented slightly to explain, 'I'm sorry, Rebel, but I can't let you do that. Not only could it wreck all our plans, but it could also prove hazardous for your brother.'

'In wh-what way?'

He hesitated and she pressed beseechingly, 'Please, C.K.! He's *my* brother. Don't I have a right to know what's going on too?'

'Well, I must admit I wasn't altogether in favour of them keeping it from you for so long,' he confessed sympathetically. 'But that's the way they wanted it, I'm afraid.'

'You mean, Chayne, Randall and Scott?'

'No, Chayne and Van,' he supplied eventually with a resigned sigh.

Rebel repeated the names to herself, perplexed. 'But I understood—from both of them—that they hadn't had anything to do with each other since Van left Mount Cavanagh. And only the other day Chayne was annoyed with Scott for having told me about your losing stock in

case I'd passed the news on to Van,' she reminded him confusedly.

'Yes, well, I think he was meaning what Van might have
said before . . .'

'Before . . .?' she prompted anxiously when it appeared
he was reluctant to further her information.

'I really would rather you waited and heard the story
from them,' he parried once again.

Now she knew where that unyielding streak in his son
came from, decided Rebel morosely. But if verbal appeals
weren't going to be successful then there were other
methods at her disposal. C.K. had reared a family of seven
sons and, with luck, wouldn't be prepared for, or immune
to, feminine ploys. With a plaintive little sniff she assumed
her most woebegone expression and unashamedly forced
misty tears into her eyes.

'It's just because I'm a female that you won't tell me,
isn't it?' she reproached in trembling tones. 'You think I
can't be trusted and—and that I'm not worthy of your
confidence.'

'Good lord, no! That wasn't the reason at all,' he denied,
appalled. 'Why ever would you think that?'

'Because if it wasn't t-true,' she faltered convincingly,
and sent him a tearfully pathetic gaze, 'there wouldn't be
any reason for you not to tell me, would there?'

For a split second he continued to stare at her closely
and then the corners of his mouth began to lift into a rueful
smile. 'I think I've been had,' he announced drily.

Rebel flushed guiltily and couldn't quite return his ironic
gaze. 'You mean you will tell me what's been happening?'
she probed, but refusing to actually admit to his claim.

'I guess I shall have to,' he half laughed wryly as he
seated himself in a cane chair. 'It would be a shame if those
arguments of yours were to go for nothing.'

She suspected he really meant her acting performance
and couldn't stop another wave of colour climbing into her
cheeks at the thought. His eyes, she was beginning to appreciate, were no less shrewd and astute than another pair

of the same hazel-green colour she was coming to know quite well.

'They were perfectly legitimate ones,' she put forward earnestly, taking the chair next to him, and wiping away the last vestige of dampness from her lashes. 'If I could be trusted, why wasn't I told?'

'It wasn't that you weren't trusted so much as you were, at that time, still an unknown quality to a large degree, even to Van. They couldn't be certain how you would react.'

'To what?'

'The role Van intended to play in the scheme, as well as to staging a dispute which would be bitter enough to convince the Lamberts he had cause to seek revenge on both you and the Cavanaghs, while at the same time providing a reason for getting you out of town,' he disclosed heavily.

Although there were a number of questions she wanted to ask, one point stood out glaringly in Rebel's mind and she sought its clarification immediately. 'Are you saying the argument Van and I had at the dance was deliberately instigated?' she gasped disbelievingly.

C.K. cleared his throat and looked somewhat ill at ease. 'So I believe.'

'And Chayne knew it was?'

He nodded, commiseratingly.

Well, didn't that explain a lot of things! 'And as if that wasn't bad enough, they've let me go on believing it was for real ever since!' she railed furiously, jumping to her feet to pace back and forth across the verandah. Her seething anger was just too much to contain while sitting still. 'Oh, I could kill the pair of them! The treacherous, two-faced, conniving...! And just whose brilliant idea was *that*?' she gritted from between clenched teeth.

'I'm not sure,' he answered quietly, soothingly. 'But as neither of them knew whether you would be capable of pretending to have such a confrontation, they apparently considered it best to play it straight.' Abruptly, his eyes began to twinkle. 'After your efforts today I'll be able to tell them differently, won't I?'

Unable to prevent her natural good humour from re-appearing with a grudging smile, it also had the effect of taking the edge from her temper, and Rebel re-seated herself with a heaved sigh.

'But they could have told me afterwards, couldn't they?' she queried, disgruntled rather than irate now. 'I mean, why couldn't Van have phoned me here and told me?'

'Because, unfortunately, party telephone lines aren't always the best way of keeping something secret, and if anyone had known he was ringing you it would have ruined the story he was trying to put across.'

'All right, so he couldn't explain,' she was willing to concede. 'But Chayne certainly could! What was to stop him from telling me? Or any of you, for that matter, since you all apparently knew about it.'

'In the main, a deference to Van's wishes. I gather he felt he ought to be the one to explain to you seeing you were his sister and he was the one who'd had the argument with you.'

'It didn't occur to him that I would have been more relieved just to know he didn't hate the sight of me, after all?' drily.

'I understood it was up to Chayne to convince you of that,' he smiled.

'Oh, yes, all those supposedly consoling little platitudes he had to offer,' she recalled caustically. 'I'm building quite a score to settle with your son, C.K. I hope you don't mind.'

His ensuing laughter was deep, pleasant, just like his son's. 'Not in the slightest. I shall await the outcome with interest.'

Rebel did wonder if there wasn't a tinge of private amusement running through his words but, not wanting to be distracted, she dismissed the idea and returned to what concerned her most.

'You said Van's and my dispute was also a reason for getting me out of town,' she murmured reflectively. 'Why was that necessary?'

'Primarily, to make good his story of wanting to retaliate

against you for your part in the argument, and against us for having taken your side, besides being a convenient manner in which to recall that he happened to have been dismissed from Mount Cavanagh not long ago,' he enlightened her soberly. 'But also, and probably even more importantly, to keep you well out of Walter Lambert's reach. They weren't taking any chances on him trying to force you into accepting his company because of Van's debts.'

'For that, at least, I do thank them,' she acknowledged sincerely, suppressing a shudder brought forth by her recollections of the man in question. 'But just what sort of retaliation was Van supposed to be planning?'

'To join the Lamberts in relieving us of our stock.'

Rebel shot forward on her chair, her eyes widening significantly. 'You mean he's ...? But how did ...? Oh, who came up with that suggestion?' she finally demanded with a hint of suspicion in her tone.

'It was Van himself, actually,' C.K. was able to divulge. 'He apparently sought Chayne out as soon as he arrived at the dance last Friday and put the proposal to him then. As I understand it, Walter had been unable to refrain from doing some bragging to him previously about how he and Morris were paying us back for not giving them the contract to renew our fences by helping themselves to a few head of our stock. As we weren't making a hue and cry about losing any cattle he put it down to just that—idle boasting—and didn't think anything more about it until the night before you arrived in Pitereeka when, after a fairly heavy drinking session, Walter brought the matter up again and was promptly silenced by Morris. By Friday night it really had Van thinking there might have been something in it, after all, and he offered his help to us in exchange for Chayne getting you out of town. After that, it was just a case of convincing the Lamberts he had as many reasons to get square with us as they did, and that a slice of the action would enable him to repay their loan in a hurry. An extremely telling factor as far as their father was concerned, so I've heard,' he concluded wryly.

'Then it was Van who Chayne's been in contact with in Pitereeka,' she deliberated thoughtfully. Suddenly a frown appeared and she eyed the man next to her quizzically. 'But if Chayne could discuss it with him over the phone, why couldn't I?'

'Because Chayne has ostensibly been checking with Denise as to how she was managing the store, while Van has been playing the role of rancorous ex-employee, divesting her of the phone and pouring a tirade of supposedly inebriated abuse down the line,' he half laughed. 'For the unsuspecting it's a jumbled mass of invective, but for the initiated there's a lot of cleverly imparted information among the double-talk.'

Rebel smiled faintly herself. It was just the sort of intrigue she could imagine Van being good at, and enjoying. 'So he'll be with the Lamberts tonight, will he?'

'We believe so,' he nodded.

She caught a soft underlip between worrying teeth. 'It could be dangerous for him if they deduce he's the reason there's a reception committee waiting for them, couldn't it?'

He was too honest to pretend otherwise. 'It could be,' he granted. 'Though there's no call to assume it will be. Besides, Chayne isn't likely to stand by and see any harm come to him, and especially after the assistance he's provided.'

Intended to allay her fears for her brother's safety, it unfortunately only served to magnify them. She loved both men, and although the thought of Chayne going to Van's defence if trouble ensued may have been reassuring in one sense, it was totally comfortless in another. It just meant the pair of them would be in the thick of things, and that was anything but encouraging to contemplate!

Late in the afternoon, Rebel made her way back to the homestead from the Metcalfes' house where she had spent a pleasant couple of hours meeting and talking with

Wendy's two older sisters and their families. They had arrived earlier that morning and their conversations had, of course, mostly centred about the forthcoming wedding.

Now, as she walked slowly around the bullock bush at the back gate—it had been another broiling hot day and there was no need for her to hurry as dinner wouldn't be for some time yet—she could hear the wheels of a vehicle drumming across the cattle grid which separated the gardens from the nearby paddocks at the front of the house and, on looking up, was just in time to catch a glimpse of a bright yellow Falcon sweeping along the red quartz drive before it disappeared from view.

However, it wasn't until she had showered and changed into a cool, soft-flowing dress of black and white cotton, and had joined C.K. and the three jackaroos in the sitting room for a drink before dinner that she realised who the Cavanaghs' guest was. Elegantly ensconced in one of the tapestry-upholstered armchairs, with a glass in her hand, and looking for all the world as if she was already mistress of the household, was expertly made up and exquisitely attired Karina Loudon.

At a guess, Rebel would have put the other girl's fabulous outfit of shell pink raw silk in a four-figure bracket, and that alone was enough to have her spirits taking a downward turn. Just how did one compete with such flawless apparel? she despaired, and completely oblivious to the unaffected grace and beauty of her own form and features, and the enviable glory of her richly coloured hair.

'Rebel! What a surprise!' Karina exclaimed, her lips shaping into a tight smile. 'When I heard you were out here to decorate Wendy's cake, I naturally expected you to be staying with the Metcalfes.'

Hunching one shoulder offhandedly, Rebel explained, 'There wouldn't have been room, so . . .'

'So she kindly consented to bring some young, feminine companionship into our male preponderant domain,' C.K. inserted smoothly as he handed Rebel her usual aperitif of sweet sherry.

'Thank you,' she accepted it from him with a smile and took a seat at one end of the sofa near the french doors so she could see the last brilliant display of the setting sun.

It was a view she never tired of watching as that line of purple-hued hills in the distance blazed fiercely red for all too few moments against the encroaching darkness, and the last patches of blue overhead became streaked with gold, black, and orange, until they too were eventually overcome by the crystal clear, star-studded sky of night.

Suddenly the seat of the sofa gave slightly and she turned to find Steve Maitland next to her, his eyes shining with amusement. 'You must be a sunset freak,' he charged amiably. 'You sit here every night and watch the sun go down.'

She laughed and took a sip of her sherry. 'I can't help myself. It's never quite the same, but it's always so unfailingly beautiful. Don't you think so?'

'It's okay, I guess,' he shrugged, and his mouth curved wryly. 'You've seen one, you've seen 'em all.'

Rebel wrinkled her nose at him in mock disgust. 'The trouble with you is you've got no poetry in your soul.'

'Oh, I wouldn't say that,' he countered lazily, meaningfully, as he took in her vivacious features. 'I just prefer to reserve my appreciation for more tangible objects, that's all.'

'Like . . . your horse?' she deliberately turned his implied compliment aside with a teasing quip.

'You would have to bring that up,' he winced. 'I could certainly have done with a bike for the work I had to get through today.'

'Well, I did tell you to go home that afternoon,' she chuckled.

'Mmm, but how was I to know the boss would come straight in to town as soon as he arrived back from the city?' He gave a rueful laugh and then sobered. 'Talking about the boss, what's he up to this evening? Hoping to put a stop to a spot of cattle duffing, is he?'

'How did you know?' she frowned. There obviously wasn't much point in denying it.

'Deduction,' he grinned. 'I was with him a few weeks ago when we moved some of the cattle out of the southern paddocks, and there weren't as many as there should have been, which immediately set the old brain ticking over—the more so when nothing much was said about it. Then we get a lot of unexplained activity on the station, which no one discusses either, and suddenly two burly coppers arrive, whereupon they all take off together, once again without any explanation. As I said ... deduction.' He grinned again.

'You haven't mentioned your suspicions to anyone, though, have you?'

'Come off it! What do you take me for ... a new chum? Believe me, I know when to keep my mouth shut,' drily.

'I—I'm sorry, I suppose I should have known better,' she apologised, remorse evident. 'I'm the only new chum around here.'

From across the room Karina's voice, purposefully loud, abruptly cut into their conversation.

'Goodness, I do believe you have a budding romance on your hands, C.K.,' she smirked. 'Rebel and Steve haven't been able to take their eyes off one another since she entered the room.'

On finding herself the partial focal point for everyone's interested gaze, Rebel flushed embarrassedly, but thankfully Steve's unflappable self-possession stood them in good stead as he shrugged nonchalantly.

'No such luck, I'm sorry to say, Karina,' he denied lazily. 'But after having to look at that pair all day,' nodding wryly towards Ben and Owen, his fellow jackaroos, 'you can't blame a feller for attempting to monopolise such attractive company during the evening.'

The older girl wagged a finger at him archly. 'Oh, I think you do yourself an injustice. Rebel seems all too willing to be monopolised by you, as far as I can see.'

Why Karina should have been going to such lengths to

insinuate there was something between them, Rebel couldn't quite fathom—unless it was just out of spite because she normally had, and expected, all the men's undivided attention when she deigned to visit—but before she could put a stop to the innuendoes once and for all, Doris came to tell them dinner was ready and the opportunity was lost. In a way, she wasn't sorry. At least if they believed her interested in Steve, there was little likelihood of anyone suspecting just who actually did fill her thoughts exclusively.

During the meal Rebel's mind constantly wandered, wondering if Van had indeed made the trip with the Lamberts, if they had arrived as yet, if there had been any trouble. Not that Karina appeared to object to her preoccupation, for she certainly wasn't averse to ensuring the conversation revolved solely around herself, and kept up a steady flow of chatter with this aim in view throughout each course. She even went so far as to be charming to the jackaroos, which Rebel noted in one of her rare moments of attention brought somewhat wry expressions to their faces, and had her guessing that when Chayne and his brothers were present it was usual for Karina to ignore the other three completely.

Afterwards, the jackaroos retired to their own quarters—as was their custom—but Rebel wasn't so fortunate and reluctantly accompanied C.K. and his guest back to the sitting room for coffee.

'So you have no idea what time Chayne is likely to return from this trap they've laid for the Lamberts?' Karina sighed, looking towards her host.

Rebel presumed C.K. must have told her the whole story before dinner.

'I'm sorry,' he shook his head regretfully. 'Although you know you're welcome to stay the night and speak to him in the morning rather than have a wasted journey altogether, if you wish.'

'Mmm, I might do that,' she condescended regally. 'However, if it wasn't for the trash coming into the area these days it wouldn't be necessary. I don't know what it's coming to when a man can't safely leave his stock in his own paddocks.' Her eyes roamed haughtily in Rebel's direction. 'Of course, someone was telling me the other day that your brother was a great crony of the Lamberts.'

Uncertain whether that was meant to imply that Van had been in partnership with the Lamberts, or was just to be included in the general description of trash, Rebel refused to rise to the bait either way and merely gave a non-committal shrug.

'I doubt anyone would classify them as great friends if they'd lost as much money to them as Van has,' she reasoned ruefully. 'In any case, I haven't seen any signs of him being on amicable terms with them since I've arrived.'

'Well, maybe he has good reason to want it kept a secret these days,' Karina smiled maliciously, saw C.K.'s darkening look, and made a judicious qualification. 'I mean, he probably realises he can't continue in the same old ways now that you're here, and we all know how rough these men can tend to become without a woman's civilising influence, don't we?'

With Van her only precedent to judge by, and having seen the mess he was living in, Rebel was hardly in a position to dispute the statement, although her acknowledging smile was perfunctorily made. It went against the grain to agree with anything Karina said.

Happily, from then on she wasn't called upon to do so any more, because Karina promptly swivelled slightly in her chair so that her back was mostly to Rebel, while she engaged C.K. in endless discussions concerning farming matters about which the younger girl knew exactly zero. Rebel couldn't really have cared less, except that she felt sorry for Chayne's father as he politely tried to include her also—only to be thwarted by Karina switching to other equally unfamiliar topics each time—and it was for his sake as much as her own that after about an hour she rose to her feet and smiled excusingly.

'If you don't mind, I think I might make a start on the

decorations for Wendy's cake. I've thought of some new designs that I'd like to try out,' she said.

'If that's what you want to do, you go ahead,' C.K. urged with an understanding smile. 'I realise this conversation can't be very interesting for you.'

'Oh, dear, I am sorry, have we been excluding you? You should have said something,' Karina cooed.

'That's quite all right,' Rebel smiled, not to be outdone. 'As a matter of fact, I found your discourse on the breeding cycle of the barber's pole worm absolutely fascinating.' From the doorway, she smiled again, pointedly. 'I was surprised you had to explain it in such detail, though. I would have thought C.K. was fully aware of its effects already.'

Doris was just finishing in the kitchen when Rebel arrived and looked up quizzically at her approach.

'Left them to it, have you?' she laughed. 'I could hear them discussing their sheep ailments when I collected the coffee tray, and thought it wouldn't be long before you'd had enough.'

'Mmm, I think I do prefer it as it's been on the other nights, with a little bit of sheep and cattle thrown in with more general subjects,' Rebel owned, glancing round the spotless kitchen. 'I was going to do some icing, but if you'd rather I didn't start making a mess in here again ...'

'No, you make yourself right at home. I'll be out of here in two seconds and then you can have the whole place to yourself,' Doris promised as she finished wiping down the sink and dried her hands. 'My books arrived from the library yesterday and I'm anxious to get started on them.' On her way to the door she paused and patted Rebel's arm encouragingly. 'Don't you let Karina make you feel inadequate with all her scientific talk, will you? She tries that on every likely-looking female who comes within cooee of Mount Cavanagh, and it's only because she's frightened to death someone is going to get Chayne to the altar before she can.'

'In that case, she wasting her time where I'm concerned, because he's treated me like a sister since I've been here,'

Rebel almost grimaced, but managed to change it to an unconcerned smile just in time.

'Yes, I've noticed how well you get along with everyone. It's been a pleasure having you with us,' Doris smiled affably. 'But now I must be going, otherwise I shall be asleep before I've finished the first chapter.' She glanced around the room experimentally. 'You know where everything is, don't you?'

'Yes, thank you, and I hope you enjoy your book.'

Rebel made up her icing mixture quickly and, armed with the piping bag and nozzles, began to try out some new designs on a sheet of plastic. Some of the flower arrangements she wanted to create were very intricate and took a great deal of time and effort to perfect, but finally she was satisfied they were as lifelike as it was possible to make them and sat back to critically gauge the total effect.

'I hope you have no objections, but I just had to come along and see for myself this masterpiece of a wedding cake everyone's talking about,' Karina's unwelcome voice suddenly intruded into the calm as she strolled into the room.

'No, I don't mind,' Rebel shrugged. She doubted whether it would have made any difference if she had. 'But I'd hardly call it a masterpiece, it's just three plain iced cakes at the moment.' She gestured towards the three gauze-covered squares on the bench behind her. 'I haven't started the decorations yet.'

'Oh, but these must be for the cake, surely?' Karina insisted, waving a hand towards the bouquets which had just been completed. Moving forward for a closer look, she clumsily pretended to stumble and, throwing out an arm to supposedly save herself, managed to flatten the delicate arrangements beneath her hand as it came to rest on the table. 'Heavens, I am sorry, they were so pretty too!' she immediately apologised in an exaggerated tone, but without being able to conceal the pleasurable shine in her eyes.

'It doesn't matter, they were only my practice efforts,' Rebel revealed impassively, even though her patience was rapidly running out. Karina's spiteful behaviour was beginning to irritate and, old family friend or not, she wasn't going to accept it meekly any more. In consequence, her gaze was sarcastic as she glanced at the other girl and pointed out, 'You seem to have missed a couple, though. Perhaps you'd care for another try?'

'I didn't do it on purpose!' Karina denied hotly.

'Didn't you?' Rebel injected a tone of innocent surprise into her voice. 'I thought you did.'

'If I had, it would be no more than you deserve!' the blonde spat, discarding any thought of restraint now. 'Just who do you think you are, coming here and acting as if you're some favoured guest instead of the glorified kitchen help you really are? I suppose you played on Chayne's good nature to get yourself invited into the homestead?'

'Not at all,' countered Rebel wryly. 'As a matter of fact, I wasn't even given a choice in the matter. If I had been, I probably wouldn't be here.'

'Hah! You expect me to believe that? I've seen the way you chase after Chayne all the time!'

'Then you've seen far more than I have,' Rebel couldn't help laughing. 'My interest in Chayne has been solely in order to get business for the store, certainly not for the same reason you're scared to give him a moment's freedom.'

A dark flush stained Karina's cheeks. 'Why wouldn't I be, when there's ingratiating little bitches like you around!' she blustered. 'It's for his own protection! He needs someone like you and that drunken, worthless brother of yours hanging around his neck as much as he does a ten-year drought!'

'But you don't think he's capable of making that decision for himself,' drily.

'I'm just making sure he does!' Piercing blue eyes glittered furiously. 'It wouldn't surprise me at all to learn the pair of you had been involved with the Lamberts in their thieving schemes. Only you were more cunning than your brother, you could see the chance of insinuating yourself into Chayne's good graces by switching sides and turning your former accomplices in to the police.' Her lips curved into a derisive sneer. 'How much are you hoping to be paid for the information, Rebel? The amount of your beer-sodden, good-for-nothing brother's debts?'

It was only with a supreme effort that Rebel managed to retain any sort of control over her escalating temper, and she needed every ounce of discipline she possessed to coax a taunting smile to her lips.

'After what you've had to say, why should I stop there?' she provoked. 'It appears I could set my sights a lot higher.'

The other girl caught her meaning immediately, infuriatedly. 'Don't bank on it, you mercenary little slut!' she raged. 'Chayne will be kicking you out of this house once I'm through telling him what your intentions are. He'll never even want to see you again, believe me!'

Rebel's shoulders lifted in a dispassionate movement. 'And if he's willing to give credence to every piece of vilification a venomous harpy like yourself pours out, then I couldn't care less!'

'*Harpy!*' Karina's eyes bulged in her irate indignation, and a violently swinging hand was launched with obvious intent.

Providentially, her intended recipient had faster reflexes and ducked, leaving said hand to sail harmlessly over her head and to connect forcefully with the back of the old wooden chair she was using instead. Karina gave a shriek which must have been heard in every room of the building and clutched the injured member to her chest.

'You'll pay for this, you see if you don't!' she gritted between lips made stiff with pain. 'By the time I'm finished with you . . .'

'What happened? Is someone hurt? I'd just put the phone down when I heard a scream.' C.K.'s tall figure appeared in the doorway, his glance anxious as it scrutinised the two forms inside.

Rebel went to speak, but this time it was Karina who was faster.

'Yes, it's my hand,' she began, turning, and plaintively holding it out for his inspection. 'Rebel jammed it be-

tween the chair and the table.' She gave a heartrending sob.
'Deliberately, I think, because I accidentally broke some of
the decorations she was working on.'

So stunned by the blatant lie that she couldn't speak
at all now, Rebel continued to sit where she was, staring
incredulously at them both.

With his forehead furrowing C.K. took in her expression, the position of the chair, and the ruined icing with
discerning eyes. 'Oh, I think you must be mistaken, Karina.
Not on purpose, surely?' he contradicted gently.

'Yes, on purpose!' she reiterated categorically as with
one last virulent glare in the younger girl's direction she
stormed out of the room.

Aware of C.K.'s glance resting on her consideringly,
Rebel selfconsciously went about clearing away the utensils
she had used with her eyes lowered.

'Okay, what did happen, Red?' he enquired wryly.

At the use of the fond nickname her father had always
used she looked up swiftly in surprise, then dropped her
gaze again with a deprecatory shrug. 'Karina told you,' she
murmured.

'I know what Karina told me, and I also know what my
own eyes told me,' he retorted, stopping her as she made
to move past him. 'Now, I'd like to hear the truth, please.'

She sighed defeatedly. 'She bumped it herself.'

'That was a loud scream for a *bump*, wasn't it?'

'Well, hit it, then.'

'But not without your help?'

'Er—not really,' she confessed, strictly truthful.

'Rebel! The truth ... remember!' he reminded her in
somewhat dry exasperation.

Her mouth shaped into a rueful grimace. 'She was—um
—waving her arm around a bit, so I inconsiderately moved
out of the way, and it hit the chair,' she relayed evasively.
She had never been one for telling tales.

'In other words, she was trying to hit *you*!' And without
waiting for, or apparently requiring, any verification,
'Why?'

'I don't think she likes me,' she quipped facetiously.

He inhaled deeply, shaking his head in disbelief as he started to laugh. 'Are you always this difficult to drag the truth from, or is it just in retaliation for my having called you Red?'

'Oh, no, I don't mind. That's what my father always used to call me,' she explained that willingly enough. 'It's just that . . .' she spread her hands helplessly, 'I don't like causing trouble, that's all.'

'Well, if there's going to be any trouble I'd rather have it caused by the truth than by a lie,' he declared uncompromisingly. 'So now will you tell me why she was trying to hit you?'

Rebel gave in gracefully. She couldn't do much else when he was doing her the honour of believing what she had to say instead of what Karina had told him.

'It was a storm in a teacup really,' she alleged, still wanting to make as little of it as possible. 'We had an argument which, unfortunately, developed into something of a name-calling contest. I guess she must have taken greater exception to what I called her.'

C.K.'s mouth levelled to an ominous line and a muscle beat steadily at the side of his jaw. 'And this argument wouldn't have had anything to do with Chayne, would it?' he demanded curtly.

'His name was mentioned.' The admittance was dismally voiced.

'In what context?'

She flinched away from the question, her head drooping in her distress. She had never heard him speak so sharply before. 'I'd really rather not say,' she whispered embarrassedly.

'When I said something similar to that to you this afternoon, you resorted to tears in order to find out what you wanted to know. As I have no intention of doing the same, what method would you suggest *I* use?'

Rebel raised her head slowly, curiously. Was he joking with her or not? One look at his face was enough to convince her and some of the strain began to leave her own tightly held features.

'I thought you were disgusted with me,' she owned with a half smile of relief.

'Not with you, Red.' He swept a hand over her bright hair affectionately, his following smile teasing. 'The lord knows why you should, but you happen to love my son. Karina doesn't, she just wants him ... like a trophy to be hung on a wall! At a guess, I'd say she told you to keep your distance. Am I right?'

It was all she could do to nod. Her brain appeared to have gone numb, and her mouth was so dry she could only speak in a strangled tone. 'How—how did you know I—that I ...'

'Was in love with Chayne?' he took pity and finished for her. An indulgent smile caught at his mouth. 'Because it's written in your eyes, as plain as day, every time you look at him.'

Those same eyes now closed in despair. Oh, God, no wonder he had taken to treating her like a sister! He was trying to tell her he wasn't interested! There were haunted shadows among the blue when she opened her eyes next.

'I didn't realise I was that transparent. I'm sorry,' she apologised stiltedly.

'I don't see why you should be. I think you're exactly what he needs.'

'Oh, C.K., that's very kind of you,' she half smiled mistily. 'But unfortunately, what you think, and what Chayne thinks, are two entirely different matters.'

'Are they?'

Momentarily, she gazed at him as if she had suddenly lost her hearing. 'I beg your pardon?'

'He's not exactly unmoved by your presence either, you know, Rebel,' she was enlightened in wry accents.

He couldn't possibly be meaning ...? No, of course he couldn't, she rejected the idea out of hand. 'Mmm, and I know what he's moved to ... exasperation and annoyance!' she relayed cheerlessly.

'You think that's all it is?' His lips twitched humorously.

'I *know* that's all it is!' she flatly refused to even consider anything else. After Chayne's attitude this morning, how could she do otherwise?

CHAPTER TEN

IT really wasn't unexpected that Rebel found it almost impossible to sleep when she finally went to bed that night. The men still hadn't returned and with each hour they were away her anxieties grew. Surely if nothing untoward had occurred they should have been back by now!

She tossed and turned, trying to dismiss the worrying thoughts, but this only served to conjure up images of Karina's malevolent features and a recollection of the lengths that girl was willing to go to in order to portray others in the worst possible light. She sighed, shaking her head, and found the pictures in her mind changing yet again. This time they concentrated on C.K. and once more she could hear him questioning, 'You think that's all it is?' as clearly as if he had been in the room with her. The words teased unendurably at her subconscious and she buried her face in her pillow in despair. No matter how much she might have wished it could have been different, she knew the answer to that question only too well!

Eventually, she supposed she must have slept, because when the sound of a vehicle door being closed alerted her and she switched her bedside light on, a glance at her watch showing it was just on three in the morning. For a moment she lay just where she was, propped up on her elbows, listening intently. But when footsteps passed her door she knew she hadn't been mistaken—Chayne and the others *had* returned—and she scrambled out of the bed and into her loosely belted housecoat.

Almost to the back door she caught up with Doris, also heading in that direction, but a second later they were both nearly knocked to the floor when Karina—her hair still carefully controlled and, Rebel could have sworn, with fresh but rather more subdued make-up covering her skin —sped by them at a half run and thrust open the screen door.

'Chayne! Chayne darling, are you all right?' she cried to the man in the lead, wedging herself close to his side and beneath his encircling arm. 'I'm so glad to see you, I've had a perfectly wretched evening while I've been waiting.'

What Chayne said when he bent his head to reply Rebel didn't hear, because just then C.K. arrived and everyone seemed to be talking at once. Nor did she look their way again. She couldn't bear to see him smiling down at the blonde-haired girl in the manner she longed for him to look at her. Instead, she deliberately turned away to search for her brother and found him beside Scott, his eyes watchful as they connected with hers, his stance anything but relaxed as he waited for her reaction. When a tremulous smile parted her lips, he expelled a relieved breath, opening his arms, and she walked right into them.

'You should have warned me,' she scolded softly into his shirt front.

'You told her?' Chayne's voice came from behind her and, tilting her head, Rebel discovered his gaze to be fastened on his father.

'How could I keep refusing?' C.K. chuckled ruefully. 'When she sets her mind to it, she can cry beautifully.'

While his sons laughed their enjoyment at his having been taken in by such a ruse, Rebel pushed her face further into Van's shirt in embarrassment, and was glad when they at last began moving inside, taking a scornfully snorting Karina with them.

'Was there any trouble?' she lifted her head to ask anxiously as soon as the others had gone.

'Not really, just a scuffle of sorts.' He laughed wryly. 'Morris never was a fighter, and for all his threatening bravado you could see dear old Walt wasn't overly keen to take Chayne on again.'

Rebel sighed thankfully. 'But where are they now?' She had only just realised the police hadn't returned to the homestead with them.

'Safely on their way to Deep Wells under lock and key.'

'Thank heavens for that! I'm so pleased it's all over at last.' She hugged him tightly. 'But I—I am truly sorry for all those things I said to you at the dance. I didn't really mean them, you know. It was just . . .'

'In retaliation for my gibing remarks? I know, love, and I'm sorry for what I had to say too,' he smiled down at her contritely. 'But I couldn't take the chance on you not being a good enough actress to carry it off if I told you beforehand what I was intending to do.' His smile became a fully fledged grin. 'From what C.K. had to say, though, I apparently needn't have had any worries on that score at all.'

'That's what he more or less said to me this afternoon,' she confessed sheepishly. 'But it was the only way I could discover the truth.'

His head angled slightly to one side, his expression half humorous. 'Were you very annoyed when you found out?'

'Annoyed? I was *furious*! I could have choked the life out of you and Chayne!'

'We reckoned that's how it might be,' Van owned drily. 'I guess I should have allowed him to explain once you arrived here, but I really didn't think it was fair to land him with that unenviable duty when the original idea had been mine. Happily though, C.K. seems to have been—um —prevailed upon to spare us both a tongue-lashing.'

'Not that the pair of you don't deserve one, anyway!' she retorted, eyes narrowing with feigned anger. 'In fact, the more I think about it, the more I'm convinced you do.'

'But not tonight, love, please?' he entreated. 'It's been a long, hard, worrying day *and* night, and right at the moment the only sound I could possibly show any interest in is the creak of bedsprings under me.'

'Of course, you must be tired! I'm sorry for keeping you

talking.' Her concern showed immediately and she began ushering him towards the doorway. 'Only you'll have to do with silent bedsprings, I'm afraid. Somehow I doubt you'll find any of the other kind at Mount Cavanagh,' she grinned.

The sitting room was empty when they passed it, but on turning into the hall they found Doris just emerging from one of the guest rooms.

'There you are, your room's all ready for you,' she smiled, and indicated the open door behind her. 'C.K. and Chayne are still in the study, but I expect you're as eager to reach your bed as Randall and Scott were theirs.'

'I think so,' Van agreed with feeling. 'And I apologise for keeping you out of yours.'

'Oh, that's nothing,' she disclaimed lightly. 'Now, you just get as much sleep as you want and we'll see you later in the day, all right?' Turning for her own room, she stopped, and looked back with a laugh. 'I forget to tell you, your bathroom's next door.'

With Van's acknowledgment given, and their goodnights said to the housekeeper, Rebel looked up at her brother happily.

'I guess I'd better say goodnight too and let you get some rest.' Impulsively, she threw her arms around his neck and kissed him. 'That's just to show I don't bear you any grudges,' she advised impishly.

Van's arms tightened about her convulsively. 'You always were the best sister a feller could ever have.'

Rebel took a step backward and smiled, but before she could reply a movement caught her attention from the corner of her eye, and on looking down the hall she saw that Chayne was approaching them. Hastily, she faced Van again.

'I'll see you when you wake up. Sleep well,' she bade him, and was nearly to her door before his somewhat surprised, 'Goodnight,' reached her.

Inside the room she paced towards the bed, her breathing unaccountably heavy, her fingers twining together agitatedly. Why she should have experienced such an overwhelming desire to avoid Chayne she had no idea. She just knew she couldn't have stayed and mouthed polite little phrases.

It took her completely by surprise when the door flew open, and her expression was startled as she spun about to find Chayne surveying her from the threshhold. Advancing purposefully, he pushed the door closed behind him.

The uninvited intrusion had Rebel's chin lifting defiantly. 'You're in the wrong room, aren't you?' she gibed tartly. 'Karina's one down, across the hall.'

A muscle began to flicker jerkily beside his mouth and his head inclined sardonically. 'Thank you, but I already happen to be well aware which room Karina occupies.'

She shrugged with simulated indifference. 'Oh, well, it was only natural I should think you'd made a mistake.'

'And maybe I have, at that!' he bit out decisively, and turned on his heel.

'Chayne!' she had called for him to stop before she even realised what she was saying. Perversely, now that he was here, she didn't want him to leave. 'I'm sorry,' she offered miserably, eyes downcast. 'What was it you wanted to see me about?'

'Forget it, I guess it's not that important, after all.' He reached for the door handle.

'No!' Rebel knew she was acting out of character in rushing across the room to interpose herself between him and the door, but she couldn't seem to help herself. 'It was important enough to have you walking in here a few moments ago, and I—I'd like to know wh-what it was,' she declared in an increasingly shaky tone.

Surprisingly, the corners of his mouth began to lift lazily, sending a wave of uncontrollable attraction rolling over her from head to toe. 'Do you make a practice of confining men in your bedroom, honey?' he drawled.

'Only when they're tall, dark, and handsome,' she attempted to reciprocate flippantly, except her emotions were too deeply involved and the words came out sounding more like a throaty endearment than a nonchalant quip.

Chayne raised a hand to finger a stray curl at the side of her neck. 'Compliments yet?' he taunted softly.

A trembling intake of much-needed breath and she flicked the tip of her tongue over dry lips. 'You—you're trying to change the subject,' she accused weakly.

'Now why would I do that?'

'I don't know.' Her voice was little more than a whisper. 'But you still haven't explained why you're here.'

'You weren't this anxious to find out when you saw me in the hall.'

'I didn't know you intended speaking to me then.'

'Would it have made any difference if you had?' The tip of one forefinger drew a gentle line along the vulnerable underside of her jaw. 'Although Van seems to have been forgiven his part in the scheme, I gather I'm not to be allowed off the hook quite so readily, hmm?'

Rebel flushed selfconsciously. 'I could hardly throw my arms around *you* and kiss you to show my forgiveness, could I?'

'It would be a damn sight more reasonable than the treatment you're reserving for me at the moment, don't you think?' An edge of exasperation crept into his tone.

Rebel's eyes closed to cover her anguish and her whole body felt as if it burnt with the heat of humiliation. Oh, God, he was warning her to keep it light and sisterly again! It was only by calling on the deepest reserves of her pride that she managed to hunch one shoulder uncaringly.

'All right, if you want to be treated like a brother,' she said and, putting her hands on his shoulders, went to kiss his as she had Van.

Only it was nothing at all like kissing Van, and although she might have persuaded her mind into thinking it would be, her emotions refused to be coerced into believing the same. The sinewed arms which held her against his lithe shape didn't feel even remotely like Van's, and nor did the hands which rested on the slender curves of her waist. There was no similarity in the width of the shoulders beneath her fingers either, or in the feel of the skin her lips were so reluctant to leave, and her brother definitely hadn't aroused this fever of riotous feeling which was suffocating her now.

Desperately, she fought to assume some semblance of equanimity. 'And now you're supposed to say I'm ...' she began, but the smouldering look in the depths of his darkened eyes, and the caressing feel of his hands through the thin silky material of her housecoat, completely annihilated her last vestige of hard-won control, and she lapsed into a shuddering silence, punctuated only by their deepened breathing.

With a smothered exclamation Chayne jerked her hard against his tautly held body and Rebel's eyes clung to his achingly, unashamedly, her head tipping back in mute invitation. Surely that fervent glow in his eyes hadn't been caused by feelings of a brotherly nature? But although she knew his heart was pounding as raggedly and heavily as her own, he still made no move to claim her softly parted lips and, in a moment of ungovernable longing, she caught hold of two handfuls of tousled hair and tugged his head lower.

'Chayne! Kiss me!' she half pleaded, half demanded, on a broken sob of restiveness.

His reaction was immediate. He swept her into his arms and swiftly carried her across to the bed where he sank down with her among the disturbed covers.

'I thought you were never going to ask,' he revealed with a groan before fulfilling her request with a sensuousness which took her breath away.

Rebel might not have understood his words, but his actions were something else, and she responded to them ardently, unhesitatingly. Pressing closer to his muscular frame, she revelled in the slow, lazy thoroughness of his mind-drugging kisses, and willingly abandoned herself to the stirring pleasure of his touch as a savouring hand moved leisurely from the outward sweep of her hip to the incurve of her waist, and upwards to cradle a ripely rounded breast.

His lips trailed tantalisingly from her mouth to the

hectically beating pulse at the base of her throat and the sweet warmth of a peach-tinted shoulder. Then, suddenly, she realised her housecoat was undone, that Chayne was releasing the shoestring ties of her nightdress, and as he slipped the concealing material downwards she began to tremble. When his mouth descended to explore the exposed skin of those gently swelling slopes and to caress compulsively thrusting nipples, she moaned helplessly, whatever little control she had had left over her senses completely lost now. It was an intimacy she had never before experienced, and the force of feeling it engendered reached to the very depths of her being.

As if sensing her emotionally vulnerable state, Chayne drew away from her slightly, a look of concern in his black-lashed eyes which had her denying its need with a tender smile and a shake of her head.

'Don't stop,' she breathed huskily, and promptly crimsoned at the wantonness of her unthinking plea.

Chayne gathered her close again and buried his face against the side of her neck. 'Oh, God, I love you, you redheaded little innocent!' he declared in rawly impassioned tones. 'But if I don't stop now, I'm afraid I won't be able to stop at all.'

It was doubtful Rebel even heard his last remark, she was too busy assimilating his first one. 'Did you just say you loved *me*?' she exclaimed breathlessly.

There was a delightful smile on his face when he lifted his head. 'Of course I love *you*! Why else do you think I'm here, instead of asleep in bed like most other self-respecting people are at this hour of the morning?'

'Oh, Chayne!' She linked her arms about his neck adoringly. 'Why didn't you tell me before? You must have known I loved you.'

'Must I?' he countered ruefully. 'Believe me, from the minute I saw you sitting in that hotel room, and looking so in need of protection, I haven't been certain of anything where you were concerned! Except, of course, to know all too well what you were doing to me, together with the realisation that you were too damned inexperienced to know you were doing it!'

'But you do know now that I love you?' She didn't want any misunderstandings about that.

'Unless this happens to be the manner in which you treat all the men you confine in your bedroom,' he teased.

'You're the *only* man I've ever had in my room,' she admitted simply.

Leaning on his side, he propped his head up on a bent arm. 'I guessed as much,' he returned drily.

She sent him a sparkling glance of provocation from the shelter of silky lashes. 'I may have led a somewhat sheltered life, Chayne Cavanagh, but I can assure you I'm not altogether ignorant of the facts of life. My thoughts regarding you are anything but innocent, if you must know,' she owned mischievously.

'Oh?' The look which leapt into his eyes had quivers of excitement racing along her nerves. 'Tell me more.'

'All in good time,' she parried with a tantalising laugh, but made absolutely no move to evade the shapely mouth which sought to plump her secret thoughts for itself. When he finally released her—and he wasn't in any hurry—she stared up at him drowsily, her finely moulded features still flushed with the warmth of desire. 'You don't fight fair,' she pouted enchantingly.

'Neither do you,' he groaned, and set his lips to the creamy-skinned valley between her breasts.

The action reminded Rebel that she hadn't yet rearranged her clothing, and she started to do so selfconsciously. When it was completed, a gentle hand captured her chin.

'You have a beautiful body, honey, don't be embarrassed by it,' Chayne urged softly. His eyes began to tease. 'Once we're married, I'm thinking of keeping you like that all the time.'

'Chauvinist!' she denounced shyly. 'Besides, you haven't yet asked if I will marry you. Or were you expecting me to do the asking, the same as I had to before you'd kiss me?'

His grin was entirely unrepentant. 'I warned you I was going to beat you at your own game, didn't I?'

'And I'm still not quite sure what you meant by it.'

'I meant, my darling little innocent, that any move to bring us together was going to have to come from you,' he smiled. 'I guessed you weren't exactly uninterested in me, but at the same time, I also suspected you weren't altogether aware—or, perhaps, ready to admit—just what was causing that interest. So I decided to play a waiting game and see if a little brotherly indifference couldn't produce the results I so badly wanted.'

As his method had proved so amply rewarding Rebel wasn't going to quibble over it now, even though she was sorely tempted to. Instead, she made do with a speaking glance which promised retribution in the future and divulged, 'Initially, I thought it was because you couldn't be bothered any more with someone who was obviously so unsophisticated. But when C.K. told me tonight—last night— that even he knew I was in love with you, then I thought you must have adopted that standoffish pose in order to let me know my feelings weren't reciprocated.'

'Oh, hell! No!' he ejaculated in dismay at the thought of such a potentially disastrous misunderstanding occurring, and pulled her tightly to his broad chest. 'Surely C.K. would have put you wise in that regard.'

'Well, he did say something to the effect that you weren't —unmoved, was the way he put it, if I recall—by my presence,' Rebel relayed, her mouth tilting obliquely. 'But as I told him, I thought that was only with exasperation and annoyance.'

'And that's the way he left it?' His brows peaked in surprise.

'No, he did ask me if that's all I thought it was ... to which I replied very much in the affirmative.'

'The old ...!' Chayne broke off with a laugh, shaking his head. 'He conveniently forgot to mention I told him last Friday that I meant to make you his next daughter-in-law, I take it?'

She nodded, starry-eyed, and smiling. 'But you hardly knew me then.'

'I waited a long time to find the girl I wanted to marry, but when I eventually saw her there were no doubts in my mind.' His voice deepened huskily. 'I've wanted you from the moment we met, you captivating little witch, and come what may, I meant to have you. So you see, there never has been a time when I *didn't* intend marrying you.'

Rebel sighed blissfully. 'And I thought you were the most dangerously attractive man I'd ever seen, but extremely unlikely to show any interest in someone like me.' She slewed around into a kneeling position, her hands coming to rest on her hips. 'Of course, I might have found it easier if you hadn't always had Karina with you!'

'I've never had Karina *with* me,' he grinned lazily, and obviously enjoying her display of jealousy. 'She merely invites herself along.'

'To wherever you happen to be! Well, from now on, if she knows what's good for her, she'll invite herself elsewhere!'

'After what I had to say in return for the stories she tried feeding me tonight, I've no doubt she will,' Chayne said deeply, reaching up one hand to tangle his fingers within the burnished skeins of her hair. 'But do you honestly believe I've got eyes for Karina when you're around?'

'You did have this morning when you arrived home,' she reminded him in hurt tones. 'You even had your arm around her.'

'Because she was clinging to my side like a damned limpet and there wasn't anywhere else to put it,' he explained drily. 'What would you have had me do, cut it off?'

She pulled a reluctantly amused grimace. 'Rather than have it around her, yes.'

His fingers slipped to the nape of her neck, forcing her head down to his. 'If I did that I wouldn't be able to put it around you either,' he murmured against her already softening lips. 'And I wouldn't like that at all.'

'Nor would I,' she assented in breathless anticipation of his closing that tormenting gap between them.

He did so with a persuasive tenderness which had her catching her breath in her throat and yearning for a more complete possession.

'Will you share my life, my bed, and my board with me, Rebel?' he asked humbly, vibrantly, long electrifying minutes later.

'Oh, yes, you know I will!' she sighed rapturously as she nestled beside him and laid her head on his chest. 'I'm hopelessly in love with, Chayne Cavanagh, in case you haven't guessed.' Abruptly, she lifted her head again and her eyes sought his with a twinkle. 'Does this mean the store can expect all of Mount Cavanagh's trade from now on?' she enquired roguishly.

His teeth gleamed in an unhurried smile. 'I'll consider it,' he taunted.

'That's what you said before!'

'And that's what I'll keep saying until I see some prices.'

She wrinkled her nose at him and then frowned. 'I've just had a thought!' she exclaimed worriedly. 'What's Van going to do with the store once we're married? He wanted to see about starting a motor repair shop.'

'Stop worrying, it's all been taken care of,' he disclosed soothingly. 'Van and I had quite a talk on the way home and everything's arranged. He's going to lease the store to Denise—who, I might add, has been in her element this week—while he gets on with what he plans to do.'

Rebel looked slightly taken aback. 'How could you have arranged it? You didn't know we were going to be married until a little while ago.'

'You forget, *I* always knew we were going to be married. It was just a matter of when,' he drawled lazily.

'Oh, is that so?' She bounced back on to her knees, laughingly indignant. 'Just for that, I might . . .'

'Yes?' Before she knew it she found herself flat on her back with Chayne's supple form leaning over her, and she looked up at him reproachfully.

'Big men aren't supposed to be able to move that swiftly,' she couldn't help smiling.

'They don't have any option when there's an enticing little redhead to be taken to task,' he laughed back.

Her brows arched expressively. 'Taken to task?'

'Mmm, like this.' He laid his lips to the unprotected base of her throat. 'And this.' He found the throbbing cord at the side of her neck next. 'And this,' as he sensuously explored her mouth.

'I see.' Blue eyes locked audaciously with hazel-green. 'That being the case, I think you're going to find you'll have to take me to task constantly in the future, Mr Cavanagh.'

'I hope so, Miss Hayward, I sincerely hope so!' he approved in loving tones.

The Mills & Boon Rose is the Rose of Romance

Every month there are ten new titles to choose from — ten new stories about people falling in love, people you want to read about, people in exciting, far-away places. Choose Mills & Boon. It's your way of relaxing:

December's titles are:

KING OF COPPER CANYON by *Elizabeth Graham*
Dani had gone to confront Grant King, but instead she found herself holed up with a disreputable character named Burt . . .

SEASON OF SHADOWS by *Yvonne Whittal*
Laura had become mother to her dead sister's child, but the girl also needed a father. Could Laura go through with a marriage to Anton DeVere?

THE LAST NIGHT AT PARADISE by *Anne Weale*
Arriving in the Caribbean to find her grandfather had died, Amalie was forced to accept the help of the mysterious Blake . . .

COMPULSION by *Charlotte Lamb*
Why was Lissa so reluctant to marry Chris? Shouldn't she be far more wary of the mysterious, reckless Luc Ferrier?

ENGAGED TO JARROD STONE by *Carole Mortimer*
Temper had provoked Brooke into declaring her 'engagement' to Jarrod Stone — and it suited him to make the engagement a real one!

DARK SURRENDER by *Margaret Pargeter*
The more Julie knew of Brad Hewson the more she realised that any woman who was foolish enough to love him was doomed to be hurt . . .

A DREAM OF THEE by *Mary Wibberley*
After the way Lachlan Erskine had treated her, Catriona had kept her distance from men — but now Lachlan had turned up again . . . .

REUNION AT PITEREEKA by *Kerry Allyne*
Why was Rebel's brother on such bad terms with Chayne Cavanagh, the man she had come to love? She just had to find out.

THE SPANISH UNCLE by *Jane Corrie*
How could Mary give up looking after her dead sister's small son when the boy's uncle, Rafael Alvarados, made it clear that he wanted him?

SOUTHERN NIGHTS by *Janet Dailey*
When Todd Gaynor took his fiancée Barbara home to meet his family, she found herself confronted with the last man in the world she wanted to see . . .

Mills & Boon Classics

The very best of Mills & Boon
romances, brought back for those of you
who missed reading them when they
were first published

In
December
we bring back the following **four**
great romantic titles.

THE BEADS OF NEMESIS
by Elizabeth Hunter

Pericles Holmes had married Morag Grant as a matter of
convenience, but she had lost no time in falling in love with
him. Whereupon her beautiful stepsister Delia, who always got
everything she wanted, announced that she wanted Pericles!

HEART OF THE LION
by Roberta Leigh

When Philippa encouraged young Cathy Joyce to elope, she
didn't know the girl was the niece of her boss, the formidable
newspaper tycoon Marius Lyon — but that didn't stop him
promptly giving her the sack. But that was by no means the
last of Marius as far as Philippa was concerned!

THE IRON MAN
by Kay Thorpe

When Kim had no news of her fiancé in the Sierra Leone she
decided to go and find out what had happened to him. And
encountered opposition in the shape of the domineering Dave
Nelson who told her, 'Don't run away with the notion that
being female gives you any special immunity where I'm
concerned.'

THE RAINBOW BIRD
by Margaret Way

Paige Norton was visiting the vast Benedict cattle empire as
the guest of Joel Benedict. She had looked forward to it
immensely, although she hadn't much liked the sound of Joel's
stepbrother Ty, the boss of the station. And when she met Ty,
she liked the reality even less . . .

Masquerade
Historical Romances

*Intrigue
excitement
romance*

A PERFECT MATCH
by Julia Murray

Louisa married Simon, Lord Winslow, very reluctantly
indeed, and she knew that he had only offered for her
to preserve the proprieties. So why should he interfere
with her innocent attempts to help his unhappy brother-
in-law, Henry Landry?

FRENCHMAN'S HARVEST
by Emma Gayle

Helen Caister agreed to visit her mother's old home —
a château in the Médoc region of France — only because
she had fallen in love with her cousin, Marc d'Auray, and
could not refuse his invitation. But Marc cared only for
his inheritance and his precious vines . . .

Look out for these titles in your local paperback shop from
12th December 1980